Barking Dogs

BARKING DOGS

Terence M. Green

ST. MARTIN'S PRESS
New York

Library of Congress Cataloging-in-Publication Data

Green, Terence M.
    Barking dogs / by Terence M. Green.
      p. cm.
    ISBN 0-312-01424-4 : $15.95
    I. Title.
PR9199.3.G7574B3 1988   87-27482
813'.54—dc19

First Edition
10 9 8 7 6 5 4 3 2 1

For Conor and Owen:
    streaks of uncanny brilliance
    and pleasure
    in the darkness:
I love you, greatly

Acknowledgments

This book, like all others, was planted and nurtured before it broke ground. Many people helped the breakthrough, and supported in various ways. For this reason, I would like to thank John Robert Colombo, Pat Cadigan, Andrew Weiner, Art Geddis, Ken Luginbuhl, Robert Sawyer, Jim Frenkel, Sharon Jarvis, Arn Bailey, and the entire East York C.I. Library staff. I would also like to thank my sons, my best friends, to whom this book is dedicated.

P A R T
ONE

Why may not that be the skull of a lawyer?
Where be his quiddities now, his quillets,
His cases, his tenures, and his tricks?
　　　　　　　　—WILLIAM SHAKESPEARE
　　　　　　　　　　Hamlet (5.1.104)

They have no lawyers among them, for
they consider them as a sort of people
whose profession it is to disguise matters.
　　　　　　　　—SIR THOMAS MORE,
　　　　　　Utopia: Of Law and Magistrates

Chapter 1

The black woman in the dark blue dress raised her hand, and Donahue acknowledged her.

"Ma'am?"

She rose as he headed up the stairs and held the microphone in position.

"I wanted to ask Pope Martin why the church is so gol-darned worried about people's sexual behavior." She nodded sharply and glanced about her. There was a smattering of supportive applause from the audience. The camera cut to Donahue's weathered, friendly face, highlighted by the perfectly coiffed silver hair—hair that, according to a group of the world's most notable stylists, ranked in the world's Top Ten. His lips pursed impishly, his blue eyes sparkled. Then Pope Martin was centered in frame, the first American pope, suntanned from his recent visit to poverty-wracked Mexico. He leaned forward, elbows on knees, to catch every word.

"I mean," she continued, "if it's only between two consenting adults, who cares? I mean, who *really* cares?" And pleased at having cut so incisively through all the theological and intellectual clutter, she sat down, nodding again determinedly.

"I care," the pope replied, simply.

In his modular Scandinavian living room, viewing with modest interest the encounter on the tube, Mitch Helwig waited for the sensation of cold, piercing steel in his left side, below his rib cage. To his surprise, it did not appear.

The pope—transfixed, transported, and transubstantiated into the electron particles on the TV screen in this year of our Lord

1999—seemed to sense that this was not enough. They want *more,* he realized.

"God cares," he added, applying invisible adhesive to his comment.

This time, Mitch did feel the tingling in his side. Not the icy shaft of pure fabrication—but merely the tingling that indicated that the words uttered were suspect. Just a tickle, a tremor from his Barking Dog.

He's not sure, Mitch realized. The pope . . . the goddamned pope himself, deep down, *isn't sure.* . . . The hairs on the back of his head prickled, and a flush of goose bumps shivered into prominence.

The goddamned pope himself, thought Mitch, leaning back, the tingling in his side receding. It was quite a revelation, he had to admit. I realize, he reflected, that the pope can't really *know* if God cares or not—not "know" in the scientific sense of experimentation, observation, and conclusion. But he has to *believe* it. He has to "know" it *intuitively.* How the hell else can he function as pope?

Mitch Helwig, who was not Catholic, suddenly felt compassion for Pope Martin. The man, he thought, somehow just got in over his head.

Like we all do.

"God knows," continued the pope, "and he wants us to understand, that the very essence of our humanity is inherent in our appreciation of the sanctity of each and every human life. Our sexuality is both a representation of and a reaction to that sanctity, and certainly our most intimate form of appreciation and communication."

Smooth, thought Mitch. He certainly is smooth.

"And," he went on, "it is not accidental that the procreation of human life is so integral a part of such a profound representation of our identities. For, in essence, our sexuality is ineluctably entwined with our Total Being. Thus, the church is not off course at all in focusing on sexuality as a potential key to Christian behavior and attitude. On the contrary, it is central to the church's theology, and central to the concept of *caritas*."

The camera switched to the befuddled woman who had asked the question, catching her alternately rolling her eyes and glaring at the pope.

Why can't he talk at her level? thought Mitch. Who the hell can follow that? It might be all bullshit—who can know? Unless they've got a Barking Dog. . . .

The tingling in Mitch's side had once again been stimulated: a rustle, like a leaf stirred by a breeze, then nothing.

Donahue himself decided to leap into the fray. He hadn't hosted this show for over twenty-five years for nothing. Timing, he had.

"What this lady probably wants to know," he proffered, extending a hand in her direction, "is whether what is morally right or wrong shouldn't be decided by what *people* feel is right or wrong—not by what someone thinks *God* feels is right or wrong." He glanced skyward and held a hand out as if expecting rain, eliciting a chuckle from the audience via his stance and expression, adding the needed comic relief to the potentially tragic morality drama he was hosting. "I mean, how can anyone be *sure* what God thinks?" he asked pointedly.

The black woman nodded appreciatively at his comprehension and good sense.

Pope Martin, the priest from Detroit who had become, mysteriously, the Prince of the Church, remained staunch. His was the first papal visage in history, this banker's son, that did not resemble that of a Balkan peasant who had suffered life's ghastliness in silence. He radiated American health, vigor, and progress. In a gray business suit instead of his ceremonial vestments, he might have sat at the head of an IBM shareholders' meeting.

"Then," replied Martin, "one would have Situation Ethics. There would be no Absolutes. What would be morally right for one person in one place and time would not necessarily apply to another person, in another place or time. The church maintains that there *are* Absolutes, that some things are Right or Wrong. In any place. At any time.''

"But how can we know what these Absolutes are?'' added Donahue.

"We have the best theological minds in the world constantly poring over these very issues. They weigh and consider, then they advise me. I, then, seek God's counsel and guidance, through prayer. God,'' he affirmed, pausing, "would not let me down.''

His smile held tremendous confidence, the certainty of blind faith. Mitch Helwig, his feet propped on his teak coffee table, felt a piercing cold stab through his vitals, where before there had been merely tingles.

Chapter 2

"There's only one way you can beat a Barking Dog,'' the lanky salesman had said. "That's if you're schizoid or mentally ill, and really believe what you're saying. It's the *belief* in what you're saying that's measured. "Crazies"—he gestured helplessly with his large hands—"believe in all kinds of delusionary nonsense.''

"And a con artist can't beat it?''

"No way.''

The salesman confronted the customer in the small store in Thorncliffe Plaza—a store that, like so many others of its ilk, had appeared suddenly and quietly on the scene. Guardian Intelligence and Protective Services. It was, the customer knew, a sign of the times. The customer was Mitch Helwig.

The salesman saw the customer frowning. "Check *Consumer Reports*'s August 1996 issue.'' Lovely, venerable old *Consumer*'s, the salesman mused. The neutral arbiter. Just mention its name and

customers relaxed visibly. It sold more units of just about everything than any other dozen testimonials. "They evaluated the top
five Barking Dogs: Sony, RCA, Quasar, Panasonic, and Hitachi.
Every one of them checked out perfectly in the Judgment Reliability category. It just can't be beaten. A con man might be a
good actor; but even he can't control his heart rate and the subse-
quent effect on his larynx."

Comforted, Mitch asked, "Ever have a dissatisfied customer?"

The salesman chuckled. "Well," he said, peering through twinkling, watery eyes, "there was one fellow. He *told* people he was
using it." He rolled his swampy orbs upward in a silent plea for
basic common sense. "Everybody stopped talking to him until he
got rid of it. But he found out one useful thing: his bookie was
cheating him. Knew the guy for fifteen years. Shows you that you
never know. He started betting the opposite of whatever his bookie
told him. So, before he stopped using it, he *made* money. Made
enough to pay for the machine!"

The customer, he noticed, was nodding. They always appreci-
ated this story. The possibility of financial insights. It hooked them
every time.

"How much again?" Mitch knew, but figured asking it out loud
might reduce the answer.

It did. The salesman also knew the game.

"I can let it go for seventy-nine hundred. Cash." He let his new
price sink in.

Mitch was sure now. Best price in town—no doubt. "Hmm
. . . pretty expensive for a luxury item."

"Luxury item?" The salesman feigned astonishment. "Sir.
Knowing the truth is not a luxury in this day and age. It's a survival tool worth whatever we have to pay for it. Like a sextant to a
sailor in ancient times!" His enthusiasm was expansive.

"These things didn't used to be all that reliable. How'd they
improve 'em?"

"You understand the basic premise, of course?"

"I know what I've read. I know they work. But the technical part, I'm not too sure of."

The two men stood gazing at the wallet-sized silver trinket, the way they would gaze at a refrigerator capable of producing crushed ice.

"All lie detectors," the salesman began, "are basically stress detectors. The precursor of this"—he gestured toward the Barking Dog—"was the voice analyzer developed by the CIA and U.S. Army Intelligence back in the time of the Vietnam war. They were looking for simpler ways of interrogating prisoners. Body odor seemed promising. Everyone gives off distinct odors under stress, but sorting them out, by themselves, proved too difficult, and often inconclusive. So, they went to voice pitch. Certain vibrations, microtremors, change when the speaker is under stress. What they devised was a device that could pick up the microtremor, the voice tremolo inaudible to the human ear. That was the start. Compared to what we have here, though, that's a Model T."

He glanced at the customer, who was listening carefully. The salesman knew a buyer. This was a buyer. This one was worth the time, he knew. He continued. "The Barking Dog is essentially a microcomputer of incredible sophistication. It *starts* with voice pitch, and cross-references it via microelectronic circuitry with body odors, face temperature, response of pupil and retina, a microwave respiration monitor, measuring stomach palpitations caused by rapid breathing under stress. It also monitors, when on video, facial expression."

"Facial expression?" Mitch's own facial expression was worth monitoring at this point.

"It has programmed into it a complex cartography that details the role of facial muscles in the expression of human emotion. The CIA and KGB investigated the area years ago. In fact, they gave it a name: FACS—Facial Action Coding System." He shrugged casually, as though it might be common knowledge. "From basic neurology, we know there are two independent pathways from the brain to the facial muscles. There's the one for deliberate expression, and one for spontaneous expression. The pathway for the former originates in the cortex; the latter, the spontaneous, is largely subcortical. The intentional cortical route leads to asymmetry in expression, while the subcortical route produces more symmetry."

"It can do all that?" Even Mitch was impressed.

"You bet it can. Each of those factors, by itself, is insufficient to produce a one-hundred percent reading. But, together, cross-referenced via the microcomputer's chart analysis, *plus* the fact that we know a lot more about the wave frequencies of the micro-tremors than we did thirty years ago, results in a well-nigh perfect reading every time." He paused. "Check *Consumer*'s again."

"Once more," Mitch said. "Give it to me once more what you do."

"Well, it depends on the situation. If you keep it in your pocket, out of sight, it still works at over ninety-nine percent efficiency. It can't scan the facial features, or check pupil and retina response, but everything else will register, providing you're within two meters.

"How about using it on the TV set, or on the phone?"

"Same thing. Some of the input will be missing, but enough will get through to satisfy it. If you hold it up so that it can scan the TV screen, for instance, it's still sensitive enough, if held steady, to get not only the facial expression, but also the pupil and retina response." He reached down and picked it up from the display case and placed it in Mitch's hand, giving him tactile contact with it, a kind of sure-fire consumer intimacy that was usually guaranteed to close a deal.

"Best place for it is in your inside jacket pocket. Then you run the wire up under your shirt and attach the sticky electrode to your side. No one knows you've got it. When someone lies to you, you feel the momentary, telltale cold in your side, and you can react accordingly. If the situation calls for it, or if it will allow it, you can take it out and hold it up directly in front of the individual.

That'll get you maximum, unblemished reading. In effect, sir, it frees you. Think of it. *Free.*"

Mitch did think of it. A lot. He liked thinking how he might use it to set things straight for Mario. What else was a partner for? Mario, he knew, would do the same thing for him. Price was not an issue. Not when it came to your partner.

He tried to get Mario out of his mind. He missed him.

"Have you got one?" Mitch asked.

"Me? You bet I do. I saved money buying a used car from a guy when he knocked two hundred bucks off *after* he'd already sworn black and blue that he couldn't go any lower." He chuckled.

"Sounds sneaky."

"Mister, when I first got into business, I thought people were basically honest. But, I'm sorry to say, there are very few people whom I trust now. You wouldn't believe the dirty games people play. Look at the stuff we sell here. There's a need for it all, and the need is growing every day."

Mitch glanced at the electronic exotica surrounding them: wiretapping and debugging equipment, phone scramblers and bomb detectors, vehicle monitors and video wrist transmitters and receivers.

The salesman put his big hands in his trouser pockets and shrugged. "Yeah, yeah, I know . . . People ask if it's really moral to use a Barking Dog. Well, the only answer I give 'em is, do you think it's moral to lie?" He shrugged again, absolving himself of culpability: a rational man who knows and accepts sharks, bacteria, government, child molesters, and earthquakes, all as part of life's sludge—part he has no control over. "You want to lie, I tell 'em, then write a letter."

He had finished his pitch. It had been a good one, he thought.

"O.K." Mitch sighed with the relief of decision. "Deal."

The salesman allowed himself the luxury of a smile. These things were hard to move, he knew, in spite of what they could do. And they could do it. But they were still priced out of sight.

This guy really wanted it, and he couldn't help wondering why. He didn't fit the profile of the typical buyer, a white-collar businessman. And the store did little walk-in business like this.

He could have had it, too, for seventy-two hundred, if he'd had a Barking Dog to use. Such were life's ironies, the salesman reflected, as they filled out the forms completing the transaction.

Chapter 3

Saddled into his skimmer on his way to the station, Mitch mulled over the "Donahue" show he'd watched. Working the afternoon shift left him at bizarre odds with the working stiffs in the mega-lithic office towers he was passing. Elaine went off to work at eight. Barbie bounced off to school shortly afterward. Alone, Mitch read the *Sun,* had a second cup of coffee, then popped on the tube from nine to eleven. "Canada A.M.": nine to nine-thirty. Today they'd had a father-son modeling team, how not to argue with your teens, aphrodisiacs, and five centenarians. "Let's Make a Deal" followed at nine-thirty. A guy dressed like a carrot traded a vacation in Marseilles for Door Number Three and ended up with a set of light green inflatable patio furniture. The sap. "Donahue" rolled on from ten to eleven.

Mitch wouldn't know how to change the routine. He didn't want to change the routine. The routine had become narcotic, somehow even more so since Mario had been killed.

The caterwauling of a Jamaican trio assaulted him from the skimmer's Blaupunkt—the latest hypo-hit, pumped to its Number One post via the New York media.

And ya love me
And ya love me in the night
And in the mornin'
In the mornin' with all yer might
So let's get blitzed
Yeah, blitzed . . .

Blitzed, my ass, thought Mitch. A wail of ecstatic anguish and tribal lust was accompanied by the beat, the beat, the beat . . .

He flipped the station to something more befitting his maturing tastes. As a soapy song from the mid-eighties slithered in, he settled back more comfortably.

Pulling into Station 52 on Dundas Street, Mitch reflected that being a Toronto cop was not what it used to be—either as a job, or for him personally. It had changed fundamentally since he had taken the Solo Option the union had negotiated in the spring.

He didn't want another partner. Not after what he'd gone through when Mario had been killed. Too hard, he thought. Much too hard.

Christ. Mitch was even little Tony's godfather.

And they still hadn't caught the punks who'd done it.

Bastards.

Blitzed, my ass. Get blitzed yourself, asshole.

I've got a Barking Dog now. No more fucking around.

None.

It was a week before he had a chance to use it the way he wanted. But he knew his time would come. He was patient.

Idling the skimmer down the lane servicing the stores on the north side of Danforth, he caught it in his peripheral vision: the swing of a beam of light across a glazed window. He cut the engine, deactivated the window, listened.

Nothing.

Adrenaline flushed through his system; his nocturnal vision sharpened.

The skimmer door swung up. He waited in the darkness, breath held.

It was there again. Then gone.

He drew his gun, caressed the trigger.

Sliding silently out of his vehicle, he approached the rear door of the store where he had seen the beam.

There it was again. He tensed.

The door had been expertly jimmied. He pushed it open, slowly, carefully, like he was moving a sleeping baby, and peered in.

As Mitch watched from the darkness, the guy rifled the cash drawer and stuffed his pockets with cigarettes and pocket lighters and trinkets and junk that wasn't fit to steal. Some poor old Greek, he thought, was losing the guts of his variety store to this punk. Look at him.

Rage filled him as he watched.

"Freeze!"

The punk froze.

"Hands on your head! Now!"

In slow motion, the thief complied, his back still to Mitch. Mitch had his gun pointed stiffly at him as he stepped from the shadows. The punk's flashlight was sitting on the counter, still turned on, providing surreal illumination to the scene.

"Lace those fingers together and don't move a muscle!"

Mitch stepped within a meter of him, holstered the gun, and withdrew his Defender. He placed the electric billy on the guy's shoulder, sliding its cool, hard surface along his neck, letting him know it was there. Letting him think about it.

"If you even twitch, even *think* about twitching, I'll bolt you so hard your brains won't unscramble for weeks."

"Hey, man, easy. I'm easy."

At arm's length, Mitch frisked him from the ankles up. He had the usual boot-knife—twenty-four centimeters, double-edged. Mitch pocketed it. In his left hip pocket, Mitch found a commando knuckle-knife: .440 stainless steel, fourteen centimeters closed, matte black handle with black Teflon-coated blade. He could slit your throat or knock your teeth out. Options. Nice. Jesus, thought Mitch, and I'm only halfway up this guy . . .

Under the punk's left arm, Mitch found the concealable shoulder holster. But what he found in it was the topper.

Mitch turned it over in his hand reverently, his brain spinning. *A laser gun*. A goddamned laser gun! The guy was a walking arsenal. Christ.

Angry, Mitch hefted it, weighed it. A Bausch & Lomb, imported. Lighter than a flashlight—burn a hole in you neater than a pin. And a creep like this has it, while we continue to be issued the police special: the same Smith & Wesson .38 that we've had for the last twenty-five years!

In his mind's eye, he saw his own antiquated weapon, the bluing worn away. Budget, they were always told. Same reason why the force couldn't spare the manpower to have everyone doubled up at all times—why they'd accepted the Solo Option.

Mario had been blown away by a guy with a .45 Magnum—after he'd been worked over with a sap glove.

Bastards, he thought. His hand began to shake as he simmered with pent-up fury.

Hitching the Defender back into his belt, Mitch stepped back. He leveled the laser at the punk.

"Turn around . . . very, very slowly."

He was hard, slight, sinewy. His mouth was a thin pencil line. About twenty-five years old. Old enough to know better.

Mitch reached unassumingly into a pocket under his bulky jacket and withdrew the Barking Dog. Holding it unobtrusively at his side, his palm facing the now wary intruder, he felt all his muscles tense, from calves to shoulders. "Did you ever kill anyone with this?" Mitch asked abruptly, indicating the exotic laser in his hand—the laser still leveled menacingly. The punk's eyes narrowed.

"No," he said.

A piercing cold shot through the wire attached to Mitch's side:

ice formed by boldness, insolence, and injustice. A glacier of terror, outrage, the crystal-cold of space. The coldness of death. Of truth.

"You fucker, you," Mitch said. When he slowly, deliberately, began to squeeze the trigger, the punk's eyes widened in comprehension of what was going to happen.

Mitch squeezed the plastic trigger. Again. A needle of light. Twice through the heart. No sound.

His mouth and eyes frozen open, the punk slid to the floor, a handful of Bic lighters spilling from his jacket pocket onto the hard linoleum with a brittle clattering.

Fucker, Mitch thought.

At 9 P.M. Mitch called home from a V-booth. Barbie's face blossomed on the screen.

"Daddy! Hi!"

"Hi, sweetheart, how are you?"

"Fine. Our class went to the circus at the Gardens today, Daddy. They shot a man out of a cannon!"

Jesus, thought Mitch, smiling. The circus. Probably the same guy who got shot out of the cannon thirty years ago when I was there with my class. Some things never change. Thank goodness.

"What else did they have there?"

"Oh, you know, lots of stuff. Elephants, acrobats, Cracker Jacks, the usual junk. But this guy actually got shot out of a cannon! How do they do it?"

He chuckled at her excitement. "I guess they use a big bullet."

"Daddy . . ."

"Don't know, beautiful. I can see we'll have to talk about it, though. You'll have to tell me all about it. Mommy there?"

"She went out right after dinner. Mrs. Chan's staying with me till she gets back."

"Oh?" Mitch was perturbed. Elaine wasn't home much in the evenings lately when he called. "Where'd she go?"

"To Jan's. Mommy said she phoned her at work and asked her to come over this evening—to talk, she said."

"O.K. Let me speak to Mrs. Chan, O.K., dear? Bye-bye. Love you."

Barbie waved and moved out of the picture. Their elderly Chinese neighbor sat in her place.

"Hello, Mrs. Chan. How are you?"

"Fine, Mr. Helwig. Yourself?"

"Good, good . . . What time did Elaine say she'd be back?"

"She said early—by eleven."

"Fine. Thanks for coming over, Mrs. Chan."

"My pleasure, Mr. Helwig. Barbie and I get along just fine. Don't worry."

"I never worry when you're there. Say good night to Barbie for me—and take care of yourself."

"Not to worry. I will."

The screen went blank.

She's out again, Mitch thought. Third night this week. And always at Jan's. Spends too much time there since Jan's marriage collapsed.

At Jan's? . . .

Sliding his hands into his pockets on his way back to his skimmer, he was delivered from his reverie by the cool, contoured shape of the laser gun there.

It was, he knew, virtually impossible to catch him. Especially with an unregistered weapon. Armed with it and his Barking Dog, the world began to emerge in clear, vivid images.

When Mitch checked out of the station at ten, the Bausch & Lomb laser was packed securely inside the shirt in his duffle bag. This goes with me, he thought. I'll find a safe place for it. Anyplace I pick is a better place than under that punk's arm.

"'Night, Mitch."

"'Night, Charlie."

"See ya, Mitch."

"Yeah. You, too."

"Oh, Mitch?"

"Yeah?" He turned to see who had called him. It was Captain Karoulis.

"How have you been getting along—Solo?"

Mitch made a tight line with his mouth and nodded. "O.K., Captain. O.K."

"Good. You're not sorry you've opted for it, are you?"

"No. You don't replace a partner so easy, you know. I want to go alone for a while."

"Mario was the best."

They were both silent. There was nothing to say.

"Anyway, just asking." He put his hand on Mitch's shoulder.

Mitch stared into his superior officer's concerned gray eyes. "Can I ask you something, Captain?"

"Sure. Anything."

"You did recommend me for promotion last month, didn't you? I mean, with your recommendation, and my record, and my grades on the exams, I've got a pretty good shot at it, don't I?"

They stared at one another.

"Mitch, I gave you the highest recommendation I could think of. Said you were exceptional leadership material. You've got a very, very good shot at it."

Mitch was prepared for it—even expected it. But the lance of insincerity was still stunningly chilling as it gored his side.

The captain's hand squeezed his shoulder with false assurance. Mitch's eyes dropped.

"But you know," the captain continued, "the competition's tough. Real tough." He shook his head, looked away. "So, promotion or not, we'll still think of you as the best!" He looked once more straight into Mitch's eyes and smiled. "Don't think about it, Mitch. It's *you* we want, not your rank. That stuff doesn't matter."

Only mild tingles now, Mitch noted. Small icicles, dripping in the spring thaw.

He shrugged. "And Mario? His wife'll get all the insurance? And the plaque from the mayor?"

"Yes, Mitch. There's nothing to worry about there. Nothing." His eyes softened.

There was no frigid signal accompanying this. At least, thought Mitch, that much is true. At least there's some decency left somewhere—for the dead.

It was probably, Mitch realized, the only reason he didn't kill Karoulis right then and there.

Chapter 4

On April 11, 1995, Mitch Helwig had been assigned a new partner. The man was shorter than he was and stockier, his handshake strong and warm. And everything about him was Italian—from his bushy moustache, curly black hair, and gleaming white teeth to the indefinable, mischievous zest. But it was the sparkle in the dark eyes that captivated him, and that captivated nearly everyone else he encountered.

Mitch, who was by nature fairly reserved, liked him immediately and considered himself lucky to have drawn him as a partner.

"How ya doin', rookie?" Mario Ciracella had said.

"It's a dog's life, ain't it?" Mitch replied.

The other man beamed, a light coming into his eyes. "Which reminds me," he said. "How do Italian dogs get bumps on their heads?"

Mitch smiled, waiting, still gripping the man's hand. In spite of himself, he began to chuckle.

"From chasing parked cars," he said, slapping Mitch's right

shoulder with his right hand. "C'mon. Let's go arrest a few extortionist jaywalkers or somethin'."

Mitch was still chuckling as they headed to the garage.

"Helwig, eh? What kind of name is that? Kraut?"

"My grandfather was German."

"Yeah? I think my grandfather was Mafioso. Either that or a priest. Defrocked."

"You're not sure, eh?"

"Who can be sure about these things? I mean, I wasn't there. Were you?"

"No, I guess I wasn't."

"See what I mean? Jesus, we take a lot of things on faith. Right?"

Mitch smiled. "Let me guess. Second-generation Italian-Canadian."

"It's that obvious?"

"The holy water's barely dry behind your ears, Mario."

Mario nodded. "My father wanted me to work with him and my brother in the construction firm. They both think I'm nuts. I think they're right."

"Ah, but do they get to wear nice clothes like these?" Mitch said, indicating the baggy pants and leaden jacket.

Mario laughed, turned, and leaned on the cruiser. The skimmers were still novel and expensive enough to be reserved for more senior officers. "I think I must've watched too much TV as a kid. Let's hope it's as interesting as at least the dullest of those shows. Remember 'Adam-12'?"

"Whatever happened to Martin Milner?"

"I think he and Jack Webb had a shoot-out and plugged one another. They're both stuffed and mounted beside Trigger in the Roy Rogers Museum." Mario's eyes were sparkling. He liked Mitch, too. This should be fun, he thought. Nice that he's got a sense of humor. 'Cause we're sure as hell gonna spend a lot of fuckin' dull days sipping coffee and mannin' speed traps. If only we should be as lucky as to have in a whole day what Martin Milner managed to squeeze into a half-hour.

"Maybe we'll end up in the Roy Rogers Museum, too."

"Which reminds me," Mario said. "How do you know when you're growing old?"

"When you join a health club and don't go?"

"Nah." Mario smiled. "When a fortune teller offers to read your face."

They got into the car for their first day together.

Chapter 5

"Mitch?"

"Yes, Captain?"

"Can I see you for a minute?"

"Sure."

"In my office would be better."

Mitch shrugged. "Sure." He followed Karoulis into the office and waited while Karoulis shut the door behind them.

Mitch waited for the captain to begin.

"Everything go O.K. on your shift last night?"

"No problems, Captain. I'm getting used to the skimmer. I like it."

"Good." He pursed his lips, frowned. "Danforth, from Broadview to Woodbine, was part of your run last night, right?"

"That's right."

"A body turned up this morning."

Mitch showed no reaction. Karoulis continued. "A Mr. Tsarianos opened his variety store this morning and found a man dead in his shop. You would have passed by his place last night on your rounds. See or hear anything?''

"Not a thing. What was the guy doing there?''

"Robbing the place, apparently. There was break and entry at the rear, and some minor contents and cash were found on and around the body.''

"Sorry, Captain. Didn't notice a thing. Maybe if I'd been on foot patrol I'd've spotted some sign of entry. But at night, in the skimmer . . .'' He managed a helpless expression.

"I know, I know. The last thing we want is one of our men alone, on foot patrol in a back alley. That's what the skimmers are for. I just wanted to check.''

"What'd the guy do—die of a heart attack?''

"No. He was shot.''

"And nobody reported anything? Nobody heard it?''

"It was a laser that got him.''

"Jesus.''

"But we don't have it. They play hell with ballistics reports, you know.''

Mitch smiled wryly. "Yeah.''

"Those goddamned things are gonna be the death of us. Be nice if, just for once, a scientist devised something that could help *us!*''

Mitch nodded sympathetically. Against his chest, he felt the comforting weight and presence of his Barking Dog. "I know what you mean, Captain.''

"Right now, it appears he was killed by an accomplice. That's all we have right now.''

"Who was the guy?''

"Small-time hood. Record as long as your arm. He's no loss. Even his parents didn't seem too upset when notified. You know?''

"Yeah. I do.''

"O.K., Mitch, that's all. Just wanted to see if there was anything you could add to the picture. Keep your eyes open.''

"Will do, Captain." He turned and walked out the door, closing it after him.

Behind him, Karoulis tilted his head at an inquisitive angle, stroking his neck, deep in thought. Then, since that was leading nowhere except to bizarre concerns about Mitch Helwig, commingled with the understanding that it was all—lasers, dope peddlers, skimmers, the commissioner's office, Ciracella's murder, street gangs, the new technology—getting away from him, slowly and surely, he thought fondly, as he always did at times like this, of his impending retirement, of a return trip to Greece. He remembered an island he had visited with his parents as a kid, remembered the sea a serene blue-green, and the winds warm, and the sky clear and sunny. For a moment he was lost again, lost between wanting to be a kid again, wanting to see his mother who had died eleven years ago, and wanting a drink.

But, he knew, he could have none of these. Not now. Not yet.

Chapter 6

Business was slightly more active on Saturdays. At least there were usually lots of lookers. The salesman, who was also the store's owner, liked to sit back and watch the lookers, trying to figure out what they were making of his wares. The older ones were generally perplexed. He was used to that. His own father couldn't make head or tail out of what he sold, or of what was happening in general in the world that would make such things marketable on a large scale. But compared to some of the bigger companies that had stepped in to fill the void, Guardian Intelligence and Protective Services was still small potatoes. At least he'd managed to get into Thorncliffe before one of the giants did some basic market research and realized it was prime territory.

There wasn't a true single-family dwelling for miles. It was all high-rises, apartments, condominiums, townhouses. There was a much higher than average influx of immigrant population, and virtually all of it was transient. Even condo ownership in the area was negligible; renting was bad enough. Something in the range of about 60 percent of all the kids were part of single-parent families. Still, it was clean—amazingly—and centrally located. It couldn't match Don Mills Plaza for potential buyers, but then again it didn't have to pay Don Mills rent.

The kids—the teens who stopped in to gaze in fascination—were generally in line and seemed to appreciate the store's goods in a way that their parents seldom grasped. This was the Gap in its latest incarnation. The world was their world. They went out in it; their parents stayed at home, with dead-bolts and security guards and video surveillance provided by the management. It wasn't much like home to people who hailed from the Philippines, the West Indies, Asia—you name it; but it was apparently the price you had to pay to establish a foothold in the Good Life of North America that they wanted their kids to be heir to. And having lived the alternative, it didn't seem unacceptable. At least they had clean rooms, hot and cold running water, and—among other wonders—cable TV and optional heated garages in winter. And the nearby Miracle Food Mart was a Disneyland.

He was watching a middle-aged Chinese couple pointing at the items on display in his window and talking in muted tones when he saw him walk in. It was the same guy who had bought the Barking Dog two weeks ago. The salesman wasn't certain if he should be glad to see him returning or not, for either he was coming to buy again or he had a complaint. At least it should break the boredom.

The salesman painted a smile on his face and wrinkled his eyes in what he thought was a friendly manner. "How are you today, sir?"

The man's eyes met his sharply. "Fine."

"And how is everything? Your Barking Dog, I trust, is performing beyond your expectations?"

"I'm quite pleased."

The salesman felt a surge of relief, and it animated him further. "Excellent! *I'm* pleased, too. And what can I help you with today?"

"I've been reading the literature on your Silent Guard and am quite interested."

The salesman showed only a flicker of surprise before adopting the professional pose of Step-Right-This-Way-It's-None-of-My-Business. "The Silent Guard. Yes, sir! I've got one in the back; wait right here." He gave the customer a confidential nod and disappeared for a moment. When he returned, he was holding an unmarked cardboard carton. Placing it on the counter, he opened one end and took it out, holding it aloft in both hands. "There she is. A beauty. Finest bit of body armor on the market today—and you can feed that statement right through your Barking Dog, sir!" He smiled.

Mitch Helwig's face lightened, and he smiled slightly in return. "I already have." He paused dramatically. "It passed with flying colors."

"That's because you, sir, have done your homework and already know the value of this item. If you're going to purchase such an item, you might as well get the best. After all, how much is your life worth? Can you afford to scrounge around for a few bucks to buy an economy model? Or do you decide that you're going to do it right, and then *do* it right?"

"You do it right."

"Good for you. Now, can I fill you in on this beauty's virtues, or are they all known to you?"

"Actually, you flatter me. I don't do that much homework. It's a habit I got into as a kid. But I do know it's ranked as the top model.''

"You must have some familiarity with protection or military fields then?''

When the customer didn't answer, the salesman moved on swiftly, realizing his error in judgment. The customer wanted to remain anonymous, and that was his privilege. Your job, he told himself, is to sell the thing, not to nose around. "O.K., then, *I've* done my homework, and you, as we used to say in school, can borrow it. The Silent Guard is a state-of-the-art body vest. Its T-shirt design is unique. It's the first successful combination of light-weight cotton and first-rate body armor. Total weight: two and one quarter kilos. There are ten layers of thirty-one by thirty-one count, one thousand denier, specially treated by a patented process. The final layer, the one that sets the Silent Guard apart from the crowd, is the solid alloy—thin as foil—that's been impact-tested to unheard-of standards. Most other vests will stop a .357 Magnum. This one, it'll stop a .45 Magnum." He let the impressive fact sink in.

"And," he continued, "the addition of the alloy foil makes the Silent Guard a viable defense against a hand laser. Lasers are strong. But they take a bit of time to burn through this baby, and if you're at a reasonably close enough range, you could rush your assailant and disarm him before any damage could be done." He shrugged convincingly. "At least it's something. Most reasonable we've come up with yet, right?"

Mitch nodded. "So I've heard."

"The Barking Dog agreeing with me?" He grinned.

"Not even a whimper."

"That should be testimony enough. I can't send you to *Consumer Reports* for these, since they've been ignored by the general public for the most part. But, if you want, I can provide the data and results from the NCPF study that set the national standard for body armor. A lot of manufacturers cut their costs by using something less.''

"Yeah. I'd appreciate that.'' Mitch knew the study's report almost verbatim.

"It's the ultimate in protection of its type. You know,'' the salesman said, "that thirty percent of all police officers that are killed in the line of duty are shot with their own or with their partner's gun. The police forces usually skip around this, regarding it as too much protection, since they can get one that'll stop a .38 for about a hundred bucks. And they're even too cheap to buy them. Cops have to buy them themselves. Funny kind of values, eh?''

Mitch knew all about it.

"Seems to me that they ignore the seventy percent who *don't* get killed with their own or their partner's weapons! What about them?'' He was actually working himself up slightly—his concern, according to Mitch's Barking Dog, quite legitimate.

Mitch knew what about them. They were dead. Like Mario, who'd be alive if he'd had one of these. He clenched his jaw grimly and his eyes suddenly became hard and far away.

The salesman was studying him, curious. But his bottom line was selling, and what happened after he sold an item wasn't his business. The world had gone nuts long ago. And all I'm trying to do, he thought, is make an honest buck.

"How much?'' Mitch asked.

"Nine hundred and fifty dollars.''

Mitch was silent.

"Best life insurance you can buy. There's more chance, statistically, if your occupation is at all hazardous, or if you need to be out a lot at night on the streets, or if you're a cabby, that you'll use this than there is that you'll need your seat-belt.''

Mitch's Barking Dog confirmed this.

"O.K.,'' Mitch said. "I'll take it.''

The salesman relaxed. He wondered what his father would say when he told him about this sale at Sunday dinner tomorrow night. Three teenagers were looking at the window, from outside, and nudging each other with interest. He fixed his eyes back on his customer. "An excellent buy," he said. "Good value."

"Anything else I should know about it?"

"No. Except maybe color."

"Color?"

"It comes in Jungle Camo, Desert Camo, Ninja Black, or Undercover White."

Mitch grinned wryly. "Undercover White."

Chapter 7

"Your turn," said Mitch, turning to Mario. Mitch had been driving that day.

"You sure?"

Mitch smiled. "I'm sure."

"Yeah. I guess you're right. I forgot yesterday, at Country Style." He opened the door reluctantly nevertheless. "What kinda donut you want?"

"Cinnamon twist."

"Ain't we got it made?" he said as he slammed the door behind him and sauntered into Honey Dip Donuts. He emerged a few minutes later carrying a white bag with a wet, brown-stained bottom.

"Careful," Mario said as he handed it in the window. "It's leakin'."

"I guess gettin' it here, all the way from the counter there, is pretty tough, eh?"

"Wise apple. Here's yours," he said, rooting around in the soggy bag he'd taken from him after getting himself comfortably settled in the passenger seat. The shotgun seat, he called it.

Mitch looked at the donut with a grimace.

"And here's the brew."

The coffee was more welcome. "Thanks."

They sat back and ritualistically opened the plastic lids, letting the endearing aroma fill the car. Tentative sips. Cops, Mitch thought. And cabbies. And bus drivers. What would donut stores do without them? An entire service industry teetered on the brink of financial collapse, he thought wryly, and we shore it up.

And then Mitch found himself thinking about Mario's better half—Angela. Further evidence, he reflected, that people matching was far too complex to be entrusted to something as simple as a computer. No one could have planned this one. As small as a minute, and twice as educated as her husband, Angela Ciracella was a teaching assistant in English literature at the University of Toronto. Mario was blatantly proud of her, and loved to toss the title of her doctoral thesis around playfully. Mitch had always assumed that there was more to the innuendo in the title than he would ever be privy to. She had called it, Mario had told him, "The Novels of Philip K. Dick: How To Find What You're Not Looking For." Every time Mario recited the title, he would add, "I'm *still* trying to find what I'm not looking for," and shake his head.

And now Angela was pregnant.

Mario tilted his head, smiled, and lilted off in his own direction. "So the doctor, see, comes out of the office where he's just been examinin' this guy's wife, see, and he says, 'I must tell you that your wife has acute angina,' and the guy says, 'I know, I know. But what's wrong with her?'" He grinned from ear to ear. Then he turned to Mitch. "You know how you know you're getting old?"

Mitch, smiling, decided to try again. "You get winded playing chess."

"Nah," said Mario, dismissing him as usual. "You know all the answers, but nobody asks you the questions."

Mitch shook his head with mock wonder. "How an asshole like

you could have done anything as difficult as have sexual intercourse is beyond me.''

Mario gave his high-pitched one-noter in quick response.

"But," he continued, "at least you had the good fortune to do it with someone of class and breeding.''

"I think it's gonna be a boy.''

Mitch smiled. "You're too dumb to have a boy.''

"Whadda ya mean, too dumb to have a boy?''

"Havin' a boy takes some planning. I read about it.''

"You read about it. Well, where'd you read about it? Eh?''

"I read it somewhere.''

"Yeah. Sure. Somewhere. In *Mechanics Illustrated*. Or in the SWAT *Weapons and Tactics Manual*. C'mon, Helwig. You're barely alive, let alone literate—let alone literate enough to read an entire article! A *book*"—he shook his head—"now *that's* out of the question.''

Mitch laughed as he watched his partner sip his coffee. "Well,'' he said, "it seems that there's androsperms and gynosperms—''

"I love it when you talk dirty.''

"And the andros unite with the ovum . . .''

"The what?''

"The ovum, you asshole, the egg, the egg!''

"Just testing you. Wanted to make sure you just hadn't memorized something from high school health class without fully comprehending it.'' He bit off a hunk of soggy cherry turnover.

"And the andros produce the boys, and the gynos make the girls.''

"I'm glad it's not the other way around.''

"But the andros aren't as hardy as the gynos, so nature balances the scales by producing more of them than it does the gynos, so that every time you blow off—''

"Hey. Watch your language! I'm eatin'.'' He continued chewing, with relish.

"You release way more andros than gynos.''

"Whadda ya mean, they aren't as hardy?" Mario was becoming interested in spite of himself. This Helwig guy sure knew some strange things, he thought.

"As soon as they're released, they start to die. They die faster than the gynos. They don't swim upstream as fast as the girlies either. And the way it works is, first one to the egg wins. So, it's harder for the boys to win. Ergo, it follows that it's harder to make a boy. Hence, it's impossible for you to have managed it. Q.E.D."

"Q.E.D., huh?"

Mitch shrugged.

"Q.E. fuckin' D., eh?"

Mitch giggled and almost choked on his cinnamon twist.

"Well, then, wise apple, how come there're so many boys around, when hardly anybody knows about who the fast and slow swimmers are?"

"Maximum penetration," Mitch said.

"Huh?"

"That's how you get 'em. Maximum penetration. That way, they don't have as far to swim. Makes sense, right?"

Now it was Mario who was smiling.

"And that's why I'm doubly sure you're not going to have a boy. Not with that little door knocker of yours. No way."

"All this from the guy with the daughter."

"Even with my vast penetration, Mario, there is still the element of chance to consider."

"Vast penetration, huh? That's not what Elaine was telling us all at the Christmas party. In fact, I learned a new word from her there when she was talking about you."

Mitch's eyebrows rose slightly over twinkling eyes.

"Yeah, Mitch. Say, what *does* 'flaccid' mean, anyway?"

It was Mitch's turn to hoot. "It means steel, Mario. Pure, un-alloyed steel."

"Steel, huh?" He reached over and took Mitch's limp, sodden

cinnamon twist from his hand and held it aloft, closed one eye, and squinted at it. Then they both laughed.

"Well, it's going to be a boy anyway."

"Why?"

"'Cause in my house, I make all the big decisions. Angela, she makes all the little ones. We got this system, see. And it works perfect."

"Like, what kind of things does Angela get to decide?"

"She gets to decide where we're gonna live. What house we'll buy. How much we should spend on it. What the mortgage payments will be. How it should be decorated." He paused. "And she decides when we need a new car, what kind it'll be, the color, and how much to spend."

"Those are the little things?"

"Yeah. Little chicken-shit stuff like that."

"What do you get to decide?"

"The big stuff." He ate the last bite of his cherry turnover, licking each finger in turn.

"Like?"

He frowned, staring deep in thought out the front windshield. "I get to decide," he said, with great dignity, "whether the U.S. should invade Costa Rica. Whether the border between Canada and the States should be eliminated. Or whether bisexuals have twice as much fun." He shrugged. "You know, the big stuff."

Mitch's smile became a chuckle and, glancing at Mario, he saw that the corners of his mouth were curling with shrewd humor, as he enjoyed his successful parry.

"And that," said Mario, "is why it's gonna be a boy." Smiling, he folded his hands across his stomach and savored the thought.

Chapter 8

Mitch couldn't decide which was more fun: the skimmer or his old motorcycle. The trouble was, they were both fun. There was nothing like cruising around on one of the department's big, dirty old Harleys, straddling it like a cowboy of yesteryear. The noise was soothing after a while. And Jesus, they were powerful. A twitch of the right hand could send you deep into the big seat, and you'd better hold on when she began to gallop. He'd only ridden the bikes that one summer and fall. In the good weather, it was like getting paid to ride something at ElectroWorld; going to work was a gas. But in the rain it was like offering yourself up as a sacrifice to insanity, sitting in the lumpy, bright yellow rubber suit, trying to avoid getting splashed by every yahoo on the roads. And the cold weather! Christ. Right through to the bone. You couldn't wear enough clothes.

Upon reflection, Mitch realized that each had its good points. But there was no question which was the more sensible, and that was the skimmer. Maybe not as powerful, certainly not as sensual or even as romantic. But a lot dryer. And a whole lot warmer.

The bikes were becoming a thing of the past, used only for ritual occasions—escorting visiting dignitaries, parades, that type of stuff. The same thing that had happened to the horse of RCMP fame, Mitch thought. Retired. Out to stud. The horse, he mused, smiling, definitely got the better of that retirement.

The skimmer was shaped like a giant enclosed snowmobile—a cross between ovoid- and cigar-shaped. It had a door on each side that swung up, so that with its doors open it resembled a futuristic hornet. Half the size of a cruiser, it could go where a car could not, and since it skimmed along its merry way eighteen centimeters on top of the surface, it was immune to the crudities of terrain, making it a hybrid of the horse and the bike. As usual, the Japanese had beaten the Americans in Detroit to the punch, and the department had ordered twenty-five as test models from the Honda plant at Alliston. Given Toronto's absurd winters, they were a much sounder investment than the mythic Harleys. Still, convenience wasn't everything, Mitch pondered irrationally, remembering the feel of the throttle in his hand.

For one-man night patrol, the skimmers were ideal.

Mitch was cruising in his skimmer now, hovering almost soundlessly down the service lane for the stores on the north side of Danforth. The lane ran for kilometers, intersected every block by a residential street; it was the same lane he had been on the night he had procured the laser.

The laser. It was still beside him, in the bottom of the duffle bag that had become a permanent part of his accoutrements, wrapped in a doeskin-soft piece of velvet that he had found in Elaine's sewing drawer. His Barking Dog was firmly attached as well, the electrode snug beneath the Silent Guard. Bulky as it all felt, Mitch nevertheless liked the sensation it afforded. He felt like he was finally equipped properly to do the job handed him—something he had never felt before. *To serve and protect,* that was the force's motto, emblazoned prominently on the sides of cruisers and skimmers. It would be a lot easier with appropriate fittings, Mitch had thought often, as had every other cop in the city. The age of high-tech is here, and we're still playing bang-bang with our .38's. Read them their rights. Get them a lawyer. They don't have one? Well, then, appoint them one. But, Captain, we know he did it. A dozen people saw him. They're afraid to testify, though. Can't we hold him?

No.

What can we do then?

You can do your job. You do the best you can. You can take pride in your own integrity. Then you can go home to your families and lead the best life you can by your example. That's what you can do. That's all you can do.

Mitch had heard it more than a few times. And it had always made a certain kind of sense. Until Mario hadn't been able to go home to his family anymore. That's where it broke down.

That's all *you can do.*

But it wasn't.

It was 10:35 P.M. when he saw him. A drunk, he thought at first as the edge of his headlight illuminated him from the knees down. Stopping the skimmer beside the prone figure, he reached for his flashlight, clicked it on, and shone it full onto the man.

He saw the blood-soaked front of the man's shirt and felt his flesh tense. Shit! The thought burst into his suddenly alert consciousness. Goddamnit. A wave of nausea, compassion, and anger engulfed him momentarily. Without even having to think about it, he cut the engine and activated the silent, flashing red light atop the skimmer. Then he let his beam of light sweep slowly in a wide circle around the perimeters before illuminating once more the man propped like a scarecrow against the wall, his head bent at a grotesque angle. There was no one else around. Reaching into his bag, he withdrew the laser and clutched it tightly. His door slid silently upward as the skimmer touched down. Mitch listened, his eyes searching.

Nothing.

Stepping out, he strode briskly to the man. Mitch felt the bile rise, then settle, as he gazed down at the gutted figure. Kneeling, he felt for the pulse of life in the neck. There it was: a throb. Another one. Very weak. Now nothing. *Come on, hang in there.* Got to get an ambulance. Fast.

Without warning, the man's eyes opened, and Mitch stared into the pitiless knowledge that a man has when he knows he will die, into the chasm that would be left when this man's final, frail struggle ended. The man tried to speak. Mitch leaned closer.

"I would've given him my money." The voice was a whisper, blown scratchingly along the pavement like dead autumn leaves.

"Who did this to you?"

The eyes wavered, darted. He was unable to speak.

Mitch, sensing the end, became more desperate. "Where were you going? Where were you coming from? Who did this?"

The lips closed, but no sound issued from them. The man tried again. Mitch put his ear against his mouth.

"The Bleeding Ban—"

The words just stopped. There was no dramatic spasming, no last sigh or gasp. They just stopped. And he died.

It was Mitch Helwig who sighed. He sighed because all his modern paraphernalia—his body armor, his Barking Dog, his imported laser gun, his skimmer—none of it was enough sometimes. Sometimes shitty things happened in the world, no matter how well prepared you tried to be, no matter how much you steeled yourself against their happening. He sighed because this man had died, and he hadn't even known him, but what had happened was wrong.

He thought of himself in his space-age projectile skimming through back alleys, a knight in the king's army, seeking dragons to slay. But the dragons would not confront him. They had ceased to be dragons. In their stead, ferrets and jackals, sharks and vultures had sprung up, scuttling away into the neon and gaudy night.

Karoulis's words came back, hauntingly. *Then you can go home to your families and lead the best life you can by your example. That's what you can do. That's* all *you can do.*

Mitch's eyes narrowed. It wasn't true, he knew. He could do more. And he would.

He knew what the dying man had tried to say. He knew the place—knew all about it.

The Bleeding Bandit.

"It must've just happened, not more than a minute or so before I got there."

"What makes you say that?" Karoulis asked.

"Because he was alive when I got there." He paused. "He died as I was bending over him."

"He opened his eyes?"

"Yes."

"Did he say anything? Anything at all?"

"No." Mitch paused again. "Nothing."

Karoulis stared at Mitch, uncertain why he felt uneasy about his officer's statements. But there was nothing he could put his finger on.

"O.K.," he said at last. "Fill out your report, Mitch. We'll see you tomorrow." Now it was his turn to sigh. "There's nothing more you can do."

Mitch's jaw tensed at this last statement.

Chapter 9

Karoulis slumped back into his chair and ran a hand through his graying, receding hair.

"I don't know, Huziak. I just don't know anymore," he said, addressing the burly desk sergeant who was still shuffling papers after depositing a hefty sheaf on his captain's desk.

"Don't know what, Captain?" His attention was mostly elsewhere. The Tigers and the Jays were playing at the stadium tonight, and he had tickets. Baseball, he was thinking. Now there's something that makes sense.

"I'm getting to the point where I don't even know what I don't know." He frowned. "I thought you were supposed to get smarter as you got older."

Huziak chuckled. "Ever read *Heart of Darkness?*"

"I don't read."

Huziak paused, staring thoughtfully at a spot somewhere on the wall off to his left. Then he tried again. "There's an old video with Marlon Brando in it that pops up occasionally on Channel 57, between midnight and dawn. . . . You watch TV, don't you?"

"My wife says I watch too much."

"Everybody's wife says that. Anyway, in it this guy travels down this river into Vietnam or someplace. The guy who introduced it said it was inspired—that was the word he used: *inspired* . . . nice, huh?—by the book *Heart of Darkness*. The movie was really weird, and I wasn't sure I understood it all, so I picked up the book at the library that weekend."

Karoulis sat back, staring at Huziak, half-listening, half-remembering something.

"Apocalypse Now."

"Yeah! That's it. You've seen it?"

"Yes."

"What'd you think?" Huziak asked.

Karoulis looked drawn, haggard. "I didn't understand it either, Huziak. But it upset me . . . it upset me a lot." He glanced sharply at the sergeant. "What about it?"

"Not sure myself. But it seems to me that the river is, like, you know, day-to-day, and the jungle is everything around us, and instead of everything getting clearer the farther we go, it just gets weirder, hazier. Like you said, I'm not so sure we get smarter either, the farther we go. Too much jungle. Too many crazies. You know?"

"Yeah. I think I know."

Huziak nodded. "The book . . . the book was O.K. But the movie . . . *it* had great music!" He paused. "Anything on that guy that Helwig found last night?"

"Nothing we can go on. Just that he was a working Joe who went out for a few beers somewhere on the Danforth. Somebody knifed him for his wallet. We don't have much manpower to pursue it too far, unless something really clear shows up.''

"What's the big draw today?"

"The usual bunch of disgusting stuff, plus a big one. We've got a seventeen-year-old girl who was dragged into a car as she stood on the corner of Danforth and Greenwood, about six A.M. She was taken to a nearby apartment and beaten and sexually assaulted. They punctured her eardrum when they let her go, and told her that if she gave them any trouble, they'd do the other one, and that'd be the last thing she'd ever hear. The only reason we know about it at all is that the mother called. The girl won't say a thing, though. We've got a seven-year-old girl who was playing in the lobby of her apartment building on Cosburn Avenue last night when a man asked her for help in finding his dog. He took her to a second-floor stairwell and molested and assaulted her. She was treated at East General and released." He paused. "Should we consider her one of the lucky ones?"

Huziak pursed his lips grimly.

"We picked up a guy in an apartment on Woodbine for sexual assault and using a knife on a twenty-seven-year-old woman who lived three floors below him. The jackass had a stocking over his head, but she recognized him nevertheless as a tenant in the building. We picked him up. Turns out he's the same character we were looking for last April—the one who attacked the twenty-three-year-old woman in the wheelchair in the same apartment block."

"A real sicko, Captain."

Karoulis indicated his agreement with a look of sour distaste. "Those are bad enough, Huziak—but listen to this." He picked up a sheet of paper from the pile on his desk and read from it. "Kay and Kay Enterprises, owners of Video Delights, retailers in erotic (and pornographic) videotapes on Broadview Avenue, were fined twelve hundred dollars yesterday in provincial court for renting a pornographic 'snuff' tape depicting a woman being dismembered and disemboweled." He looked up. "A 'snuff' tape. A depiction of real sexual murder. And they fine the owners twelve hundred dollars. I wonder what the judge would have done if it had been his daughter? Eh? What do you think?'' He dropped the memo into the wastebasket.

Huziak looked suddenly older himself. "A twelve-hundred-dollar fine.'' The words slipped weakly from his lips.

"Boy, we really know how to stick it to them, don't we?''

Huziak nodded knowingly. "That's why the courtroom cheered when they sent Rodgers up for life, last month.''

"Yeah. But how often does that happen? And how often do we have evidence of that type, all videotaped, down to the last, minuscule atrocity?''

"Not too often.''

Karoulis grunted his assent.

"And they're on me about the drug situation, as if I can do anything about it—anything that'll really count. Jesus. The streets are floating in anything you want that'll get you high—that'll pump your courage up enough to do something disgustingly barbaric so that you can get the bucks to get your next hit. It's a circle, and we're running around inside it.''

Huziak sat down in the beaten leather chair opposite the desk. The captain, he realized, was really worked up this morning. He was always passionate about the need to do one's best, but it seemed to have slipped beyond that this morning. Something was bubbling to the surface from some deep, dark well. Perhaps, thought Huziak, I shouldn't have mentioned that Brando movie.

"They clamp down in Miami, so the boys in Bogotá reroute it through Toronto, where it filters down into the States. You plug one leak, and it springs out somewhere else. I really wonder what the hell we're doing. You know?''

Huziak gave him a minute to control his breathing, to let him simmer down. The captain wasn't that far from retirement, he knew. And from what he was seeing and hearing this morning, it might be sooner than he thought. "Was that the big one you mentioned, Captain?''

"Huh?'' His eyes focused once more on the sergeant.

"You said there was the usual assortment of worms, and something big."

"Oh, yeah. Christ. I almost forgot. How could I forget?" He put his hand to his forehead. "Listen to this, Huziak. This one's a beauty. A dilly." He was breathing heavily and shaking his head. "It's war, now, Huziak. That's what it is."

Even Huziak, used to the exaggerations of his captain, felt worried about what he was seeing and hearing this time. "What is it, Captain?"

"The government was storing six thousand—did you get that: six *thousand*—laser guns at the Moss Park Armory at Queen and Jarvis. Westinghouse, GE, imports, you name it, they were there."

"*Were* there?"

"They're not there this morning."

Huziak's eyes widened.

"They disappeared overnight. Six *thousand* of them. They found seven guards locked in a room there. All dead. All with a neat burn-hole in their foreheads. Four trucks are missing. It was a professionally executed, streamlined operation."

The two men stared at one another.

"There are six thousand lasers out there this morning, Huziak. Six thousand that weren't out there yesterday. Where do you think that leaves us?" A vein in his temple throbbed visibly.

For a moment, Huziak could think of nothing to say. "I don't know, Captain. I don't know."

"Neither do I." He sat down, touched his index finger to his cheekbone, let his eyes dart nervously around the room, and exhaled like a man who has gone too far down the river into the jungle.

Chapter 10

Mitch Helwig was on a four-on, three-off rotation. He had waited for Thursday to come along, waited with an intensity that had not been noted at the station by any of his colleagues. But Elaine had picked up some of the vibrations, and so had Barbie. There was no disguising it at home.

He squirmed and scratched, skimmed through newspapers and magazines without taking in anything, had to be dragged joltingly into conversations, and picked at his food. But it wasn't until dinner on Thursday, on his first of three days off, that it came to the fore. Elaine had gone to elaborate pains to produce a fine meal—pork roast, potatoes, candied carrots, salad, even a bottle of white wine—and was assiduously, yet tentatively orchestrating a solid attempt at a traditional family dinner and discussion.

Mitch was in another world.

"Daddy!"

He stared at Barbie, seeing her for the first time that evening. He had summarily answered questions, and metronomically smiled and nodded in most of the right places. But he had finally been caught at it. Looking into his daughter's face, he realized it—realized that the adult will tolerate the blandness of procedural etiquette, beaten into the formless mold of societal and economic dictates, but the child will not. At least not this child. And just as suddenly, he felt a rush of warmth for the pixie figure that was his eight-year-old daughter, smiled, and knew that at this moment, she was right and he was wrong. He was wrong to have ignored either or both of them. He had to give them this much. He had to.

She was frowning, doing her best to imitate her mother's most exasperated expression.

"What is it, sweetheart?"

She sighed and rolled her big eyes around helplessly. "You weren't even listening, were you?"

"I guess I wasn't. Not really. I apologize." He glanced sideways and caught Elaine's eyes on him, a puzzled look on her face. "But I'm listening now. Really—I am. There's just so much going on at work that I'm not with it sometimes, dear." He shook his head theatrically, as if clearing cobwebs. "Now . . . You were saying?"

"I was *telling* you about the circus. You *said* you wanted me to tell you all about it. Remember?"

"I remember. Did you think I could forget?"

She looked at him suspiciously. He smiled disarmingly.

"Well," she continued, "the whole thing was kind of incredible. I mean, all those animals and everything. How do you get to be an animal trainer?"

He looked surprised. "You don't know? Why, you enroll in an extension course at Humber College. You can learn anything there—duplicate bridge, self-hypnosis, Japanese finger-pressure massage, lion-taming . . ."

"Daddy's teasing, dear," said Elaine.

"In the old days," he continued, "you had to run away and apprentice yourself to someone with a heavy Austrian accent and muscles of iron . . . and a brain to match."

Barbie giggled.

"But it's so much easier nowadays. Everything's so much easier. Just take a course." He sipped his wine, glanced across at Elaine, who was relaxing, pleased at the fact that he was with them once more.

"Sure, Daddy, sure. Right."

"Actually, the training for dealing with wild animals starts by being a parent. If you can get your kids through to age sixteen, lions are nothing. Pussycats."

"It starts by being a wife, Barbie. If you can get through sixteen years with your husband, lions are a delight," added Elaine.

"*I'm* beginning to think it starts by being a kid. If you can get through sixteen years with your parents—especially you two—you'd be ready, that's for sure."

"It was the guy in the cannon that interested you, isn't that right?"

"Yeah. That's right! Why would anyone let themselves be shot out of a cannon? *I* sure wouldn't do it. Would you?"

Mitch paused, pretending to be deep in thought. "I guess it would depend on what they paid you, wouldn't it?"

"They could never pay me enough, that's for sure."

"How about if I said I'd give you a thousand dollars to let me shoot you out of the cannon at the Gardens?"

"No way."

"But it's been tested. Never had a serious accident. A little hearing loss maybe."

Elaine laughed. "And you talk with a slight stutter afterward. But what the heck, eh?"

"Exactly. What the heck."

"You guys are crazy."

"What about you, dear?" Mitch asked, smiling at Elaine. "How much would they have to pay you before you'd let them shoot you out of a cannon at the Gardens?"

"I think the guy at the Gardens probably has it made. I mean, he's got a net and people applaud after he does his job. He's two up on me there. What do you think, dear?" She stared at her husband long and hard, smiling, and finally sipped some wine.

Barbie sat silently, glancing from one to the other, understanding that the levity had disappeared, somehow, without fully comprehending exactly how it had happened.

Mitch's face became serious. But only for a moment. Then the twinkle returned, forced to the surface by a superhuman effort on his part. They all continued eating.

"I hope," Barbie said, breaking the silence, "that he has earplugs at least."

Mitch finished loading the dishwasher, then broke the news to Elaine. "I'm going out for a bit this evening."

"Oh." She turned, looked at him. "Where?"

"Restaurant, down on the Danforth." He straightened the cutlery in the drawer.

"But we've already eaten. Or didn't you notice?"

He smiled. "I'm going to meet a guy there."

"Who?"

"Just a guy. A guy who might know something about—about what happened to Mario."

"That's out of your hands now, Mitch. You know that. It's being handled by detectives, by Homicide. It's got nothing to do with you anymore."

Mitch's eyes hardened. He had made the story up, in order to leave the house with a minimum of fuss. But hearing how it had nothing to do with him anymore sent spidery tingles of outrage through his brain.

Suddenly, he found himself in a bizarre kind of impassioned defense for his imaginary rendezvous—triggered by Elaine's dismissal of his responsibility. "It has everything to do with me. Everything. Anything I could learn would be helpful. Those bastards down at headquarters have come up with nothing, a big zero, and the longer it sits around, the farther back it gets shelved."

She watched him in silence as he breathed heavily, watched his jaw muscles tighten, noted the distant ice in his eyes, and understood. She could not agree. But she understood and knew that she should say no more. A lot more time was needed to heal this wound. What her role in it all should be was the dilemma—a dilemma she would have to continue to sort out by herself—as we sort out all dilemmas, inevitably, she thought.

"I'm sorry."

His eyes were still far away. But he heard her. He was coming back.

"Just don't be gone too long. O.K.?" She touched his hand. He heard Barbie flipping the dial on the TV in the living room. "O.K.," he said.

Chapter 11

Mitch Helwig scarcely turned a head as he surreptitiously slid into the Bleeding Bandit just after eight o'clock. Blue and orange electric lights were the prominent illuminants, and the smoke and noise enfolded the patrons like a sleeping python. The throb of electricity was the lifeblood of the bar, its power, its identity.

On his belt, partially concealed beneath his open, cotton jacket, Mitch had hooked the Barking Dog, hoping that it could get enough video input from there to prick any balloon. Even without it, he knew he would slice through the bullshit in a way that Station 52's finest could never hope to match—at least, not until they started fighting back with adequate artillery, he thought.

He walked unassumingly to the bar, sat down. The bartender approached, a youth with pointed spikes of green and yellow hair and a curving row of fake diamonds glinting from his left ear. He waited for Mitch's order without speaking.

"Molson Lite."

The youth reached into a cooler beneath the bar and produced the beer and a glass, and moved off down the mahogany sleekness to the far end, where he conversed in muted tones with a trio of similarly attired and groomed males. Mitch tilted his glass and drained the bottle into it, letting the foam rise, then settle. He sipped some from the top. It was cold and biting and good.

Squinting through the gloom, he surveyed the room, noting only about twenty or so people throughout. It was still early.

Off in a corner, a stripper, better looking than the place deserved, gyrated in the glow of blue and orange, her breasts tilted to show an artificial fullness, her thighs quivering on that fine line between the sensuous and the jouncy. She was duly ignored by most, who in turn duly ignored one another; this was not a spot where one went to be noticed. It was, in fact, quite the opposite. People got lost here. On purpose.

The music—a touch too loud and a lot too shrill—oozed from the twin speakers hung like grotesque bat wings in each corner of the room, the audio accompaniment to the video flickering riotously in the lounge's most remote nook.

He sipped at the cool brew again.

The bartender approached, weaving to some personal, unheard beat, carrying an empty glass.

"Excuse me."

The youth glanced at him with cold, dilated eyes.

From his jacket pocket, Mitch extracted the photo he had lifted from DeMarco's desk in Homicide yesterday. He flashed the snap of the man who had breathed his last words into his ear on the cold pavement of the alley not too far from here. The man's eyes were closed—society's concession to propriety.

"You ever see this man before?"

The youth glanced involuntarily at the photo, then back at Mitch, then shook his head.

"Yes or no?" Mitch wanted the words.

"No." He put the glass in a sink, stared at Mitch with the blank expression of a computer, and left to rejoin his peer group.

Mitch pocketed the photo. Nothing. No howling from the Dog. He placed an elbow on the bar and continued to sip casually at his beer, his eyes and senses alert.

After about five more minutes, he picked up his glass and

walked directly to the trio of males that were bobbing and weaving to the beat of the electromusic stinging through the bar. They saw him coming and formed into a defensive semicircle, their constant-motion frames becoming ominously still.

The bartender glanced at him, then at his pals, knowing what was coming. Mitch held the photo out for them to see. It drew their eyes like a magnet.

"Any of you guys ever see this man before?"

They glared at the photo, interested in spite of themselves. One by one, they shook their heads, dismissing him. Mitch needed more. He would have to force it from them. He was beginning to understand the pragmatics of force.

"You?" he asked, suddenly, swinging the photo in line with the one on the far left.

"No, man. I told you, no." He grinned inanely.

"How about you?" He addressed the next one, a youth of about twenty, who had painted his eye sockets yellow, then rimmed them with purple.

The youth grinned defiantly. "The dude looks dead. I know lots of dead folks."

"Him?"

"Never had the pleasure, my man." The grin widened.

"How about you?" Mitch held it out two feet in front of the third youth. Haunted eyes, peering from browless sockets, glanced at it, then at him.

"You a cop?"

"No," Mitch lied.

"Who is he?"

"He's my sister. He had a sex change operation."

The youth smiled, eyes glittering. "Don't fuck with me, man."

A small trickle of fear seeped down Mitch's spine. But he couldn't let it show. Weakness was what they waited for. He had seen it many times. "Yes or no?"

"Maybe."

It was the truth. The Barking Dog was as quiet as a graveyard.

Mitch's adrenaline began to pump. "Where? Where have you seen him? When?"

The youth continued grinning, and glanced at his comrades, who picked up the grin like a spreading wave, letting his dependence on them wash over them in some minute token of victory.

"What's in it for us?" It was the one with the yellow eyes, graphically limned.

"There's nothing in it for you, bright eyes. You never saw him."

"How do you know?"

When Mitch dismissed him by turning back to the boy with no eyebrows, the youth's mouth twisted contemptuously. "Don't tell him nothin', Sten. His sister was ugly anyway."

He began to laugh under his breath at his joke, and the bartender and the first youth joined in, anxious to be a party to any form of baiting, no matter how vicarious.

But the hollow-eyed youth with the "maybe" was lost in his own world of drug-induced pleasure. A simple yes or no would have halted the game. The boredom that had led to their barroom habitat might be temporarily displaced, if he could play cat to this mouse a bit longer. He glanced at the others, saw the dim lights dancing crazily in their eyes, knew that they too were bored, and that he could establish some form of prestige by setting up the mouse with the picture here.

His eyes swung out and scanned the small crowd in the lounge. Then they stopped, fixed on two men at a table off in the arcade corner.

Mitch followed his gaze, noting well where it fell. He, too, saw the pair.

"I think you should ask Eddie."

"Eddie who?"

Hollow-eyes nodded to the table with the two men.

"Jumpin' Eddie." The other three laughed.

Jumpin' Eddie was indeed his man.

It had been mere days ago that he had sat here and watched the

man that Mitch had come upon in the alley. He had noted that the
man was not dressed in leathers or bright cottons like the rest of
them, that he was dressed instead in the casual clothes of someone
who lived around here—jacket, open-necked shirt—and had wandered in for a few drinks.

A mark. A fly. An angelfish.

Easy chewing.

He had watched the few drinks become several, seen the fist-
ful of bills flash every time another couple were dropped at his
table.

Probably just had a spat with his old lady, thought Eddie. Or
maybe his teenage son just spit in his eye or wracked up the car or
wants to spend the weekend at ElectroWorld with his buddies. Or
his boss has pissed him off, again. Or maybe just a walk on a mild
autumn night.

It was idle speculation, and it ricocheted in a disjointed fashion
through Eddie's weakened synaptic connections, taking only a second or two.

The bills flashed again. Eddie twitched and danced inside his
sinewy body. His own old man, he remembered, would never give
him the car. And he had spit in his old man's eye. But his old man
never hit him, because Eddie had told him that if he ever did, he
would kill him.

He recalled the fear in his old man's eyes.

Eddie's only regret now was that he had not killed him.

When his prey rose to leave, Eddie reached into his pocket and
tripped the switch that was wired to his ticklers. He had one
clipped to his back between his shoulder blades, where it could
literally send a shiver up and down his spine. The other was con-
nected to the thimble attached to the baby finger of his left hand.

Eddie rose and followed him.

On the street, the stranger turned north.

The mouth of a service alley beckoned ahead and to the right.
Eddie's grin widened.

Reaching into his pocket, he withdrew his skinner. It fit snugly

into the palm of his hand, its handle nonslip, shock-absorbing neo-
prene. From between his index and second finger, the three inches
of hollow-ground razor-sharp edge broadened to a lethal spear
point. With it resting softly in his fist, Eddie felt invincible and
deliciously powerful. He had seen it work—seen how it could
effortlessly slice through major muscles with only a deft movement. Much of what he had seen, in fact, had been his own hand-
iwork.

Eddie reveled in the eventual submission of his prey, and in his
mind he saw his father, again, forever and always.

"Hey," the stranger said, frightened now. "Hey, you don't
have to do anything. You don't have to hurt me. You want
money? Take the money. Okay? Okay? Here . . ."

The man pleaded with him to take the money and go—to leave
him alone with his terror and mortality and shame and helplessness.

"Yeah," Eddie said. "Yeah, I don't have to hurt you, do I?"

Cars in the distance. A horn honked.

Eddie looked into the man's eyes.

Saw the fear.

Then he plunged his right hand into the man's stomach and
ripped up as hard as he could. When the Skinner grated against
breastbone, he stopped and stared into the stunned horror that was
etched onto the man's face, stared into the questions that would
have no answers, into the face of the man whose last visual image
would be that of Jumpin' Eddie Stadnyk's grinning, self-indulgent
visage.

Mitch watched the youths warily now, watched the glee that his
plight had induced in them, tempered his actions and words by
slowly pocketing the photo and moving away from them, carrying
what was left of his beer over to the table that had been indicated
with such malicious delight. He was, he knew, being observed
with pleasure from behind.

Eddie Stadnyk, who had been shooting the bull with long-time loser Lionel "The Loon" Santos, debating the merits of shoplifting and straight break-and-entry, watched the man approaching them with the cunning and guardedness of the electric eel that he was.

Mitch hovered over the table with his glass in his hand. "I'd like to join you." He sat down without waiting for a response.

Eddie's body recoiled like an eel sliding backward into its lair. Only his fangs were left at the ready, as one hand went to the skinner in his pocket, caressing it like a woman.

"Do we know you?" The Loon's eyes were dull and dangerous. "No."

"Why don't you fuck off, then," Eddie added poetically. The lethal spear point of steel peeped from the closed fist inside his jacket pocket.

Mitch stared at them, then stood up. "O.K." He had decided, from experience and training, that he was too close to the pair. And besides, by standing, he gave the Dog a chance to see them when they spoke. If they spoke.

Slowly, so as not to spook them, he brought out the photo, placing it on the beer-stained wooden veneer of the table.

"Ever see him before?"

The Loon gazed at the picture blankly. "No," he said. "Who wants to know?"

"You?" Mitch addressed Eddie.

Against his better judgment, Eddie glanced at the picture. It took a second or two for recognition to flare. It would have been instantaneous if the man in the photo had had his eyes open, because Eddie had paid special attention to his eyes.

"Never seen him before in my life."

The Dog burned him with a searing cold, howling with indignant outrage at the boldness of the lie, and Mitch knew that he had struck pay dirt. It had worked. He felt giddy for a moment.

He sat down again, watching them tense. From the corner of his eye, he could see the delight of the grotesque quartet that had steered him here, and knew that they were anticipating, with ghoulish relish, his submission and perhaps even his demise—here or elsewhere—tonight.

"I told you I've never seen him. What do you want?"

Mitch could see that the speaker had his hand in a pocket, so he put his hand in the pocket of his own pants and clasped it about the secure shape of the laser there, pointing it through the material in the general direction of his potential antagonist.

"If either of you fuckers even blink too quickly, or even give me a look I don't like, the laser that's aimed at you under the table will separate your balls from your body, and you'll be instant geldings, watching them bounce around your stupid feet."

Nobody moved.

"Understand?"

Eddie licked his lips, carefully. The Loon remained frozen.

"How do we know you got a laser under there?" It was Eddie's last attempt at bravado.

"Try me."

The minute ticked by. Blue and orange electric chords hung in the still air like a matrix for their tension. A video game whirred as a cybernetic missile pierced hyperspace, and the floor vibrated dully with the electrobeat that was everywhere.

For the first time, the Loon looked truly worried. Now that he understood the possible danger, thought Mitch, this one was even less dangerous than before. His strength came from his brute stupidity and the lack of regard he had for his own potential pain and injury. It was the one called Eddie he had to concentrate on now—Jumpin' Eddie, they had called him. Mitch could see why. He was strung out on something, eyes dilated, his little mouth twitching. Dangerous. Very dangerous.

Mitch didn't take his eyes off him.

"Whadda ya want?" asked Eddie, finally.

Mitch himself was pulled taut. "I want you guys to get up. Then I want you to walk ahead of me out the door and onto the street. Then we'll take it step by step from there. Any sudden moves, I kill you both." He paused. "Or worse."

Hollow-eyes was watching curiously from across the room.

"Move. Now. Quietly."

Eddie and the Loon rose slowly.

"And take your hand out of your pocket or I'll leave it in there permanently."

There was only a second's hesitation, then the hand appeared, balled into a tight fist.

Mitch rose from his seat. "Let's go."

Eddie glanced over at Hollow-eyes and the group at the bar. Mitch's eyes followed his line of vision, then jerked back to the two before him.

"You'll never get out of here. We've got an audience." Some of Eddie's confidence was returning.

"You mean *you'll* never get out of here, if any of those flycatchers come over here. Think about it."

Eddie was obviously thinking about it, letting the possibility run through his little mind like a rabbit through long grass. He didn't like the odds at all.

They began to move toward the door.

Hollow-eyes moved laterally to meet them, reaching the door a few feet ahead of them. "Eddie, my man. What's happenin'?" In the same instant, a butterfly knife, with a twelve-centimeter skeleton handle appeared in his hand, as casually as if he had been unrolling his fingers from an entertaining bit of legerdemain.

For five seconds nothing happened. Sounds of steel and smoke curled lazily about them. Nobody moved.

A pencil-beam of blue light appeared with no warning, one end attached to Mitch Helwig's pocket, where a small burn-hole blossomed darkly to three centimeters in diameter, the other attached to Hollow-eyes's knife hand, hitting the soft flesh of the palm just below the wrist. His mouth and eyes widened in shock, and a yelp of crystallized pain escaped from his white lips before the knife could even fall from his shaking fingers. In the same instant, Mitch's right leg shot out and kicked the youth full in the crotch, doubling him over, dropping him to the floor, where he shrank into the fetal position, eyes and mouth still wide in soundless shock.

Eddie and the Loon remained frozen. Behind him he saw a scrabbling of random, mostly defensive, movement. But no one came forth. No one challenged.

"Move!"

This time they moved, no questions asked.

Outside, they strode briskly along the sidewalk, the darkness covering them like a blanket.

Chapter 12

Elaine Helwig sat numbly in front of the family computer monitor. Nothing had prepared her for this.

There was over ten thousand dollars missing from their savings.

Her mind could not, for a moment, even form coherent thoughts. *What had happened?*

She saw the numbers. She thought of Mitch. She thought of his behavior this evening—his behavior, in fact, for quite some time now. I know, she thought, that all marriages go through high and low periods. That's only logical. In the realm of human affairs, nothing travels on a steadily inclining plane. There are always going to be periods of time—sometimes extended periods—when you have to simply ride it out. That was what she believed. It was what she had seen, by example, even in her parents' marriage. When things got rough, you thought of the family, you put it all in perspective. There was more at stake than your own convenience—always.

But there were limits. There was always a limit.

She and Mitch had never been able to afford a home of their

own; they had been content to live in the Thorncliffe apartment complex. For ten years now. Not owning a home was something they had gradually inured themselves to. They had both abandoned the newlywed dream, accepted the unreality of such a goal, given the unbreachable gap between their incomes and real estate costs. It was one of the reasons that they had limited themselves to one child. They had both felt that raising a family of more than Barbie—once they had her and realized what was involved in terms of energy and commitment—was unrealistic. And she hadn't minded, not really. There were compensations.

One of them was that they had some extra savings—savings that other families ended up sinking into their homes, in one way or another. She and Mitch had seen graphic examples of it: Shirley and Jack's new roof and family room; the Perlmans' new paved driveway, lifting the sunken front porch; the second-mortgage payments, the taxes, the upkeep, the insurance, the you-name-it. Over the decade of their marriage, they had managed to amass, proudly, twelve thousand dollars, all of which, they knew, wouldn't amount to much if applied to the purchase of a house.

So they had other things instead—things that alleviated the pressure that could accumulate when you finally buried a dream. They took nice vacations. They ate out more often than most of their friends. Mitch never decried any money that Elaine spent on her own clothes or grooming, saying that it was a small price to pay for a wife so lovely. He also knew that if these things were taken away, life, in its unrelenting monotony, could close in on them mercilessly, suffocating the occasional gasps that made life memorable. And he had an unwavering faith in his wife's good sense, and knew that she, too, understood all this and would never do anything so outrageous as to tip the balance and throw the finely tuned way they could both deal with life out of kilter.

Until now.

Without consulting her, Mitch had spent—somehow, on something—most of their life's savings.

For Elaine Helwig, it represented an irrevocable break with the past. This had been *their* money; they had both contributed to it, both seen it grow, and always discussed major expenses or purchases. It was the only way.

Until now.

Mitch had gone out. Where? What was happening?

She scarcely let herself think it. Another woman? An array of convoluted scenarios swept through her brain, marching into dim, faceless corners, making her head spin in disbelief.

Yet, how could she disbelieve it? There it was—in white on green readout—the cold equations of financial truth.

The money was gone. So, tonight, was Mitch.

For the first time in her life, Elaine Helwig could see no part of the future with any certainty.

Nothing.

And it left her more alone, more isolated than she had ever thought possible.

Chapter 13

"Where you takin' us?"

"You'll recognize the spot, Eddie. I have a feeling you'll know it."

He led Eddie Stadnyk and Lionel "The Loon" Santos ahead of him as they turned north off Danforth and headed toward the mouth of the approaching, darkened alley.

"In here."

The two slowed apprehensively. The Loon was scared, but with his limited wits he lacked any alternate plan of action, so obeyed unhesitatingly. Eddie was scared, too. But he was scared in a different way—in the way that made him truly dangerous. Fear made his adrenaline pump faster, seemed to sharpen his mind; he used this edge to keep him going, waiting for the moment when the man behind them would relax his guard, however minutely, and he might turn the fulcrum of power in the opposite direction. It kept him going, this belief that eventually he would gain the upper hand, and he fantasized the moment and its succulent aftermath. Eddie had been in tight spots before, and it had never occurred to him that a spot might appear that could squeeze him dry and shake the husk. So he watched. And he waited. And for him, time seemed elongated, and everything transpired in a blackly lyrical slow motion of suffused, violent potential.

The lone street lamp was a high, distant glimmer when they finally stopped, and shadows spun off into darker shadows, embracing one another with the starkness of urban geometry.

Mitch eased the laser out into the open. "Turn around."

Eddie and the Loon turned and stood, unmoving.

"I'll kill you if you move. Understand?"

The Loon nodded anxiously, his dull eyes crazed. Eddie waited a strategic moment, then nodded, much less dramatically. His whole body was a steel wire, ready to garrote this stranger who had been so brash, so open. He stood still, waiting.

Mitch opened his jacket at the waist, letting the Barking Dog see and sniff and fix on the two before him. The gesture was lost on them, since the wallet-sized unit was anything but obvious, especially in the muted light that cast a pall upon the wearer.

Mitch looked at Eddie. "You killed him, didn't you?"

Eddie did his best to look perplexed. "Who?"

"The man in the photo. The one I showed you."

"I don't know what you're talking about."

The cold lanced into Mitch's side, shaking a fist at the speaker. Mitch actually felt a tingle of anger course through him.

"You killed the man in the photo, didn't you? You gutted him and left him here—right here—to die."

Eddie said nothing.

"You did, didn't you?"

"No. I don't know what you're talking about."

The frozen icicle speared him deeply, seeming to enter his vitals, where it lodged and refused to thaw.

For Mitch, it was better than a signed confession. He turned his attention to the Loon. "And you, asshole. Were you there, too? Did you help this scumbag gut that man? Eh?"

The Loon's eyebrows shot up and he twitched with fear. "No . . . I don't know nothin'. I never seen the guy before. Honest!"

It was the truth, Mitch realized. He had just snared this man in his net when he gathered in Eddie. *Jumpin'* Eddie, he reminded himself, glancing at the killer's lean, sunken cheeks. Should he throw this fish back, he wondered, returning his attention to the Loon? Or was there some advantage in having him here, flopping about on deck, gills snagged in Mitch's skein?

He was definitely a keeper, Mitch thought, relying on the intuitions developed on street corners, in back alleys, in blue arcades, and in shakedowns over the years. He could be wrung and shaken.

"You ever kill anybody?" Mitch asked softly.

The Loon glanced quickly at Eddie, then back at Mitch with a cauterized expression.

"Answer me."

The Loon licked his lips. "No."

Another stab of cold, one that spread far up Mitch's side, slowing only when it reached just below his armpit.

"Ever kill an unarmed, defenseless man or woman or"—Mitch hesitated—"child?"

"No. I said no. What do you want from me?" The eyes could not stay still.

The receding cold was struck by another wave that sent a kind of surf spray of shattered ice bits cascading as far as Mitch's now-heaving chest. Christ, he thought. I've got a pair of them here. Can I do it? Can I do what I know I must do?

But not yet, he realized. Not yet.

Then he reached into his pocket again and withdrew the other photo he had there—the one of Mario. He had to try.

"You." With a nod, he indicated the Loon. "Take this. Carefully," he added, "and look at it closely."

The Loon reached for it with pudgy, perceptibly shaking fingers, and brought it close to his eyes in the dim light.

"Ever see him before?"

The Loon squinted, then shook his head. "Who is he?" he asked.

Eddie butted in. "Why should we answer your questions? What are you lookin' for?"

Mitch turned to stare at him. "You should answer my questions because then, maybe, just maybe, I won't kill you. At least"—he shrugged—"it's a chance, right?"

Eddie showed no reaction. But the words got through to the Loon. "Here, Eddie. Take it. Look at the man's picture. Go on. Look at it. Maybe we can help the man, then he can let us go. C'mon."

Mitch backed up a step as the photo changed hands, the laser poised.

Eddie, too, gave the photo his cursory examination.

"Ever see him before?"

Eddie shook his head, then said, "No."

Nothing from the Dog. No prowlers.

Mitch felt mild disappointment. It had been too much to expect. He had done well enough simply by stumbling upon these two sewer scuttlers, he knew. To have gotten an I.D. on Mario would have been like winning the lottery.

Out of the corner of his eye, Mitch saw a ten-meter-long laser of light appear instantaneously from the direction from which they had just come, its origin in the shadows, the killing end on his chest. To the astonishment of its operator, instead of slumping dead to the ground, Mitch spun his arm and fired his own Bausch & Lomb at the other laser's source. The beam of light sprang into life, thin and lethal, and tracked onto his assailant. The laser that was trying to burn through the Silent Guard blinked out of existence, and Mitch heard it clatter to the cement pavement, along with the voiceless sound of a dropping body. Still stunned, Mitch glanced at the smoking hole in his jacket and shirt, amazed that it had worked. In the instant of distraction, Eddie Stadnyk was lunging toward him, his skinner rigid in his right hand.

Mitch cut him down with a laser through the forehead, tumbling him forward in a heap at his feet.

Then he turned, breathing heavily, and pointed his shaking hand at the Loon. "All right, you scumbag fucker," he said in a rasping whisper, through bared teeth. He was prepared to do it, aching to do it, finally. The entire light show of blue arc-beams and death had consumed no more than five seconds, but Mitch felt like he had lived his lifetime in that eyeblink, and the surge of life that ran through him now was like a volcano that could engulf the entire city with ease.

In total silence the lasers had danced in the darkness, eerie visuals that left behind a wake of afterimages imprinted on their retinas, white-hot streaks that faded with the slow exploding-snowball effect of a series of flashbulbs going off in a dark room.

Mitch's hand trembled.

The Loon licked his lips; his hands jerked with nervous twitches at his sides.

They waited. Total, awful silence.

Mitch was calming, gaining slow control of the wash of adrenaline that had raged to every extremity of his body, channeling it cannily into a heightened sense of awareness and predatory shrewdness of his own. On the force, one never saw oneself as a hunter, stalking, closing for a kill. The years of training, the years of civilizing combined to temper the ancient instincts, to shroud the primordial beast within. But thousands of years of evolution did not disappear easily; indeed, they did not disappear at all. They were merely cloaked—thinly. The right prod, the precise danger, and there were no more laws, no more trappings of civilized man. And what could sometimes emerge was more basic, more true, even more necessary. He saw the cowering, shuddering figure before him as a wounded animal, a dangerous one—both to him and to his kind. He glanced down at the laser in his hand and knew that the rules were changing, that technology and human cunning were accelerating far beyond the feeble pace of the lawmakers and the politicians, outdistancing them the way a starship approaching light-speed could outdistance the moon shuttle, about to bolt into hyperdrive and disappear from sight, perhaps forever.

"The picture that I showed you . . ."

The Loon's ears perked up.

"The second one. It was of my partner. One of you fuckers killed him."

"It wasn't me. I told you."

"Who?"

"I don't know. Honest."

It was the truth. Mitch knew this. The rules had changed.

"Who could tell me about it? I want a name."

"I don't know."

But there was a waver, a tremor that tickled the Barking Dog. Mitch seized it like a terrier taking a rat. "You're lying. I'm going to kill you."

"No. No. Don't do that."

Mitch steadied the laser on the Loon's heart.

"No!"

Mitch waited. The Loon sweated, eyes frantic, nearing hysteria.

"You're dead."

"I'll give you anything. What do you want? You want money? I can get you money."

With his left hand, Mitch touched the Barking Dog on his belt. "See this?"

The Loon squinted at the silver rectangle.

"It's a Barking Dog."

The Loon's eyebrows rose up. He needed to hear no more. He licked his lips again.

"I want a name." Mitch paused. "Understand?"

The Loon nodded.

From the Danforth, the squeal of tires rent the air. The only other sound was their breathing.

"You've got thirty seconds."

"I can't. They'll kill me."

Mitch shrugged.

They waited.

"Time's up."

"No. Wait."

Mitch aimed the laser with great care.

"I don't really know his name."

Mitch waited. It was true.

"You gotta believe me."

"Belief has nothing to do with it. I'm not some asshole district attorney, not some little old lady conscripted for jury duty. The game has been thrown out the window. Don't you get it? There's just you and the Dog. I merely pull the trigger when the answer is wrong."

His eyes jumped like a trout on a hook. "Then you know that I'm telling the truth. You know I don't know."

"I know you don't know a name. But what do you know? A face? A place? What?"

"If I tell you what I know, you have to let me go."

"Don't be such an asshole. I don't have to do anything. You assholes watch too much TV, too many game shows. You think the world works along the lines of 'Let's Make a Deal'—that you can trade everything for Door Number Three and maybe you'll hit the jackpot. Make the deal and you get to go back to mugging and killing and raping and stealing. Game show mentality. You poor simple fucker."

"Why should I tell you then? Anything?"

"Because I'll kill you if you don't. You can count on it."

"You could kill me anyway."

"And that wouldn't be fair, right? And fair is the operative word here, right? You're a pig and a moron to boot, but even a moron needs to have a carrot dangled occasionally." Mitch sighed. "Give me something good, something the Dog can accept, something that might lead somewhere worthwhile, and I'll think about your future. I'll give you that. I'll think about it."

The Loon almost relaxed. It was something. He couldn't believe the guy would do him, right here and now, if he played ball with him, at least a bit. Mitch had been right. Although the Loon could never have articulated it that way, he did subscribe to the barter mentality. It had worked for all of his dull, brutal life, and he relaxed because it was one of the few things he understood. Play ball with a guy who's got something on you. Give him a soft, fat pitch right up the middle. Then bide your time before tossing the beanball at his skull. It all worked that way; only the chumps, the fish saw it otherwise.

"There's a warehouse. There's guys there. They know everything that's going down. Somebody there might know."

Mitch's Barking Dog accepted it.

"Where?"

"North of Thorncliffe. East of Laird."

"What's the address?"

"Don't know."

"How will I know it?"

The Loon was silent for a minute, trying to decide how much information was too much. Then his eyes strayed back to the Barking Dog gazing coolly at him. If the guy kills me, he thought suddenly with unusual clarity, then he kills me. What do I care what he does after that? But if he lets me go, then I'll kill him. Eventually. Or one of the boys will, once I put out the word. And I don't think he'll kill me.

"I was only there once. To a meeting of sorts. It's kind of a stash place."

"What's stashed there?"

"Whatever needs stashing. Stuff that needs to be fenced. Stuff that needs to be stripped or doctored before sale."

"Quit fucking around. How will I know it?"

"I told you. I was only there once. But I do remember the name of the place. It was Herrington Storage, or something like that."

It had all filtered through the Barking Dog without incident. Suddenly, Mitch felt tired—bone weary. The tension was draining out of him, leaving him completely rational and able to weigh all the alternatives, without the addling effect of anger or fear.

He looked at the Loon, who was also relaxing visibly, feeling the trade had been accepted, that the man in front of him was too ordinary, too sane and well-balanced to be the threat to his life that he had been a few moments ago.

"Let me go now. I've told you everything I know. I'm no good to you now." The Loon waited.

"You're right. You're no good to me now."

The Loon smiled weakly.

"You're no good to anybody, ever."

The smile faded.

"The rules have changed."

A frown crossed the Loon's face.

Mitch squeezed the trigger evenly. The Loon's mouth started to open. It was the last deliberate movement he made. The blue pencil beam bridged the gap between the men instantaneously, flaring to life, burning silently through the Loon's heart. He fell to the pavement like a puppet whose strings have been unceremoniously dropped, his head bouncing hard on the tarmac.

You got Door Number Three, Mitch thought. It happens to all of us, sooner or later.

He stared down at the two bodies, feeling nothing. Then he strode over to the third victim, the one who had brandished the surprising laser from the darkness. It was Hollow-eyes. Bending, he retrieved the laser from the ground near his assailant's outstretched hand, slipped it into his pocket, and walked with a steady gait out of the alley. He didn't look back.

Chapter 14

Elaine heard the front door lock turning and glanced at the bedside clock. 12:11 A.M. There followed the soft sounds of the light-weight steel door opening and closing, the whisper of the deadbolt sliding home, and then moments of silence before the bathroom door clicked shut.

The digital clock blinked to 12:12.

Water was running into the bathroom sink. The sound was familiar, comforting. It meant Mitch was home. It meant an end to her solitude. It meant the possibility of continuing. She had decided that much. They had too much together to open an unbridgeable chasm right now. If it was going to happen, well, it was going to happen. But she would not instigate a midnight confrontation. Mitch, she knew, needed many things right now, and she hoped that one of them was still her.

The anger and fear and depression that she had felt earlier in the evening had dissipated. In their stead was a strange—strange to her, at any rate—acceptance of this turn of fortune. The idea of one's life's savings was in itself a curious one, she came to realize, if it was measured on a computer printout or on a monitor, as a plus or minus balance, no matter how many zeros were involved in the final figure. Elaine thought of Jan and how her collapsed marriage had riddled her with anxiety, guilt, depression, in spite of the fact that she was well-supported by the separation agreement. The numbers didn't add up to the total involved. It was the emotional equation that needed balancing.

The water in the bathroom stopped running.

This man she lived with, whom she both knew and did not

know, with whom she had shared everything worth sharing, was the man she wanted to live with. It was her choice. It involved no one else, except their daughter, and that too had helped fix her mind on its present course.

Mitch came into the bedroom with his shirt and jacket in hand, bare to the waist, his hair mussed and wet. She saw the beginnings of his middle-age belly appearing, in spite of the fact he was in excellent shape and not even forty. Seeing it made her feel good, because she could remember how it had once been taut and a source of pride for him, and the fact that the memory was hers, that she had been privy to the graceful change, linked her to the past and anchored her sternly.

"You awake?"

"Yes."

"You didn't have to wait up for me."

She shrugged. "Couldn't sleep."

He unbuckled his pants, slid them down and off, and draped them over the back of the chair—the same chair he always draped them over. Then he slid his briefs off and walked naked to the closet and took down his pajama bottoms from the hook inside the door.

Elaine let her eyes linger pleasantly on his nakedness. "Hey, you," she said, suddenly.

He looked up, his pajama bottoms still in his hand. The expression on his face told her that his thoughts were still somewhere very far distant.

"Can I interest you in a bit of salacious conduct?"

Their eyes met and locked, the communication total, the result of ten years as man and wife.

Elaine's heart was pounding. This was the moment of a certain kind of truth. Her nervousness came from the fact that her words had sprung spontaneously from her lips, completely unplanned. But only after they had left her, after they had spilled out into the world, never to be recalled, did she realize where they could lead. They could lead to the truth, the truth she had sworn she would not seek, at least not tonight. For if there was another woman, and he had been with her, his body would be unable to withhold the truth from her. A physical resonance blossomed from their ten years together, and she felt she could read his responses like a coded cipher, and translate the signals unwittingly.

The words were out. She could not get them back.

Mitch gazed gratefully at the woman in his bed, the woman he needed more than he could ever know. His body responded and he felt his manhood swell slowly but surely.

She watched him drop his nightwear to the floor, and her eyes, unbidden, were magnetized by his swelling erection. A sense of relief flowed almost orgasmically from her as she both relaxed and tightened simultaneously.

Mitch walked across the room and sat down on the bed beside her. He stroked her hair gently, brushed her forehead, her eyebrows, her nose and lips with the feathery tips of his fingers. Then he slid his hand onto the fullness of her breast, feeling the nipple harden and tense beneath her nightgown. In turn, she reached out and took his hardened manhood in her hand and caressed it lovingly.

Mitch gasped now at her knowledgeable ministrations, and the fire burned in his veins and in his brain. Bending, he kissed her full on the lips, and the kiss grew into a mutually ravishing exploration as the kindled spark was fanned, as it spread like a bushfire toward a devastating conflagration.

When, eventually, he entered her, it was with ease, so great was the tension in both of them, and the lovemaking transpired at a pitch only a fraction below that of frenzy. When, as was their pattern, her orgasm had overwhelmed her, left her floating far beyond the confines of their insignificant apartment, and he felt he could no longer contain himself, the eruption that claimed him was without precedent.

His body blew apart.

The apartment blew apart.

And he drained himself in great, wracking spasms, internal convulsions, and nerve-shattering siphoning, giving his mind and body the relief they needed beyond all others, in the arms and body of his wife.

Elaine's eyes welled with water as she listened to his gasps and felt his torment leave him. Whatever it was that had isolated him from her of late, that had prompted him to act alone in the matter of their savings, it was not, she now felt with certainty, a woman.

And with that knowledge came a relief that drained her equally.

Chapter 15

"Read me this morning's goodies, Huziak. I'm sitting down." Karoulis pried the plastic lid off the white Styrofoam cup and let the hot coffee steam out into the small office.

"We've got some arrests, Captain."

Karoulis's eyebrows perked slightly. "Good," he said, simply. "Start off with the good news. Give me some hope first." He tried to sip his coffee, found it too hot, placed it back on the paper napkin, and merely held it for warmth and comfort.

"We picked up James last night. In a flophouse on Shuter."

"He come peacefully?" Karoulis couldn't believe it.

"We surprised him. He had no choice."

"Good."

"I think we'll make this one stick, too."

"Christ. We'd better."

"We've got the witnesses. Can't find the guns he used, though."

"We release him after three years on an attempted murder charge. His slimeball of a lawyer gets him off of the murder rap in '94. We suspect he's raped his mother as well as beaten his wife as well as killed the family of ten. . . . We fucking well better have the bugger this time!''

"And," Huziak forged ahead, trying to ignore the captain's outburst, "we've got a suspect in the homosexual-related mutilation slayings.''

"Who?"

"Guy named Berskis. Stanley Berskis. Age thirty. A house painter.''

"Wasn't Hitler a house painter? Standing on that ladder all day must drive you mad.''

"The guy was wanted in Lake County, Illinois, and in Indiana. He was released on bond in February when his bond was reduced from one million to ten thousand dollars after a judge ruled that evidence uncovered in Indiana could not be used in court.''

Karoulis held his head.

"Berskis's neighbors told us he attracted attention to himself by leaving his apartment drapes open and walking nude in front of the window.''

"So he comes here and gets himself a nice apartment and carries on.''

"Appears so.''

Karoulis sighed. "And that's the good news.''

Huziak pursed his lips, nodded.

"Well, now that I feel so much better, I guess I'm ready.''

Huziak cleared his throat. "Yes, Captain.''

"Don't dally, Sergeant. Let me have it. I'm strong.'' He smiled wryly and placed his hands behind his head and sat back, waiting.

Rolling his eyes, Huziak continued. "We had four major break-ins overnight. A total of $256,875 estimated take. Thieves took $150,000 worth of bakery equipment from the Delphi Bakery on Pape. Jewelry, a camera, and a purse valued at $35,000 were taken from an O'Connor home. A side window was forced. $30,000 in jewelry and clothing was lifted from Danny's Imports on Coxwell. And jewelry and household items valued at $28,000 were taken from a Gamble Avenue home.''

"I didn't know anyone on Gamble Avenue had that much of anything."

Huziak shrugged, still refusing to be drawn in by his captain's pique.

"We got a woman walking with a friend to 'cool off' after a quarrel with her boyfriend, who was subsequently abducted, held captive for twelve hours, and raped by as many as twenty men. The woman, Thelma Maher, forty-one, and a nineteen-year-old girlfriend were walking to breakfast after the woman had just finished arguing with her boyfriend when a car containing three men pulled over. One man tried to grab the younger woman's purse. She ran away, but the victim was thrown into the back of the car and taken to a Dundas Street East apartment, where she was repeatedly raped. Apparently, a number of people passed through the place and it became known that she was there. She escaped twelve hours later by slipping out a door. She was naked when she flagged down a passing motorist—a woman—who told her to hide in the backseat of her car and drove around looking for a police cruiser or skimmer. McMahon brought her in."

"Can she find the place again? Can she I.D. anybody for us?"

"That remains to be seen. Let's keep our fingers crossed."

Karoulis nodded. "O.K. What else?"

"Nothing more on the missing kids."

Karoulis was silent. There seemed to be one missing every week. They never turned up.

Huziak decided to use his lighter material. He had been saving it for a finish, but sensed that the captain might need it a lot right now. Come to think of it, he realized, I can use it, too. "You'll like this one, Captain."

"Oh? I thought you'd given me my good news for today already."

Undaunted, Huziak continued. "Seems a couple of early-bird employees arrived at about seven A.M. this morning at Brownwood Medical Clinic, on Parliament near Gerrard. They could hear a voice shouting 'Let me out!' and a pounding from inside a wall, so they called the fire department. The fire fighters arrived, kept shouting to the trapped man, and he responded by pounding and shouting back so they could reach him. Eventually, they cut through the plaster and into a sheet-metal duct that measured about twenty-five by thirty-five centimeters to find this guy. He had evidently lowered himself into the air vent after climbing on the roof last night, and gotten himself stuck good." Huziak smiled, and Karoulis found himself responding with a small kind of perverse pleasure. "We got him now. Larry Hughes, twenty-three, of Sumach Street. Breaking and entering."

"Good."

"Ain't it though?"

"What was he after?"

"The usual. Drugs. Pills. Small-time dealer who was going to pull the perfect caper. Must've seen it on TV."

"So now they're in the walls themselves." Karoulis shook his head. "It used to be termites, you know. Not people."

"Or carpenter ants."

"Aren't they the same thing?"

Huziak looked perplexed. "Not sure, Captain."

"Hmmm." He looked up. "That it?"

"No, sir. Got another dandy."

"You're in rare form this morning, Huziak."

"Not me, Captain. The world."

Karoulis sipped his coffee. It was finally consumable. Part of him preferred merely to hold it, to smell it, to take comfort from its regular appearance on his desk as a talisman of order and routine.

"It started about five A.M. this morning and finished up about seven-thirty. Haven't you listened to the radio?"

"No. I like quiet in the morning."

It occurred to Huziak to say that he was in the wrong job for that, but prudence came through once again and he remained silent on his own thoughts. "It was up in the Thorncliffe apartments. Some sixty-two-year-old guy who was mad at everybody in the world tossed most of his possessions out of the sixteenth-floor window of his apartment. It began at five, when he threw out his mattress, TV set, and French-style antique telephone. Fire fighters were called again. They used loudspeakers to warn him, but he just wasn't in a listenin' mood." Huziak read from a list now. "He threw away cameras, picture albums, food, full cans of beer, pots and pans, piles of newspapers, telephone books, pornographic magazines, a set of encyclopedias, mayonnaise jars, a box of batteries, two bicycles, a half-dozen new bicycle tires, and new and used clothing. He tossed pillowcases, pens, and sets of suspenders still in their packages." He glanced up, curious to see Karoulis's expression. He wasn't disappointed. Even the perpetually grim captain was allowing a trace of a genuine smile to exhibit itself, however slightly.

"He couldn't very well do all this quietly, could he?"

"No, sir, he couldn't. In fact, he amassed quite a crowd of onlookers, all of whom appeared much more delighted than appalled. In fact, Citypulse News, channel fifty-seven, had cameras there for live coverage, and preempted regular programming. Some in the crowd gathered below shouted, "Refrigerator, refrigerator!" and he pushed the apartment's refrigerator out the window to the sidewalk sixteen stories down. The flights of the refrigerator, the apartment stove, and other large pieces of furniture brought whoops of glee from the crowd."

Karoulis sat with his mouth open.

"A few yahoos called out for the guy to jump, but cooler heads prevailed and hushed 'em up."

"How'd it all stop?"

"Well, officers were called in, but were reluctant to break into his apartment for fear he might be armed. Eventually, he was talked out. Nobody was hurt."

"Poor bastard."

"Hmm?"

"Poor old bastard." He seemed lost in thought. "What'd we do with him?"

"Took him to East General for observation. We got hold of a niece who said he'd been despondent since his wife left him twelve years ago."

"And we put the guy's misery on TV, eh?"

"Misery sells."

"Everything seems to sell."

There was a quick rap on the door and they both looked around to see DeMarco, Homicide, staring in at them through the glass-partitioned door. Karoulis waved him in.

"Sorry to interrupt, Captain."

"That's all right. What is it?"

"Just in. One of our men has been shot."

"Oh, no. Christ. Who?"

"You probably don't know him too well, Captain. Transferred from Peel County in the spring. Name's Fedwick. Mark Fedwick."

"What happened?"

"He answered a break-in alarm at Adamo Computers Peripherals, Inc., and Stanton Telecom, Inc., on Wicksteed, about six this morning."

"Six in the morning?"

DeMarco looked up from the paper he'd been reading from. "Pretty incredible, isn't it?"

Karoulis sighed. "Everything's incredible."

"We figure they'd been in there most of the night, but only near the end made the mistake of triggering an alarm."

"The place cleaned out?"

"Just about."

"How bad is Fedwick?"

"Critical. It was a laser, Captain."

Karoulis's face sagged.

"He was hit at least three times in the chest, and twice in the arms. It looks as though he threw up his arms to protect himself after he took the first shot in the chest. The doctors think the other two shots to the chest came after he was lying on the ground. The burns are, they say, more intense in those two.''

"And he's still alive?''

DeMarco nodded. "They missed the heart. But,'' he added, "they got just about everything else. The admitting doctors figured the aorta'd been nicked. Also, the liver, a lung, a kidney, bowel. He also lost a finger when he was shot in the arms.''

Karoulis's eyes widened. "We're looking for animals!''

"Yes, Captain.''

"Any family to notify?''

DeMarco glanced down at his notes. "Fedwick was divorced. Forty-nine years old. Three children, though—daughters, all grown. He was one year from retirement, if he wanted it, Captain.''

Karoulis felt the anger rising in him, the fury of impotence in the face of this type of slaughter.

"His gun was still in his holster, Captain.''

"I want the area blocked off.''

DeMarco looked stunned.

"Call Peel. Ask for reinforcements. And North York. Even York County.''

"I don't think we've got the manpower, Captain. We'd need two or three hundred men!''

Karoulis's eyes had hardened. He swung his gaze back to De-Marco. "Then ask for volunteers. Get on the phones!''

DeMarco hesitated, looked at Huziak, who had remained silent throughout. "I don't know, Captain, if the union allows for this type of volunteering. I mean, suppose someone gets hurt or something? What kind of compensation, insurance, is in effect? You can't—''

"Get on the fucking phones, and get on them now! I'll take all the heat, you hear me? I want that fucking area sealed tight! Mount Pleasant to Leslie; Eglinton to O'Connor. We'll stop every car. All police are to be armed with shotguns, you hear? If we can't get enough men from those on duty today from the forces, then start calling off-duty men and putting it to them, understand?''

''Off-duty—''

''Would you stay at home and have a second cup of coffee if you were called and asked to come in to help collar the killer of one of your colleagues? Would the union rules be an issue?'' He was breathing hard now, his jaw clenching.

DeMarco pulled at his ear and dropped his eyes.

''Put it to them! Try it!''

Huziak left the room, heading for the phones and shouting names. Heads turned and listened as the news broke.

DeMarco looked from Karoulis to the activity out on the floor, then back. He smiled weakly and nodded in compliance. ''Maybe you're right, Captain. Maybe you're right. Maybe it's time to break a few rules.''

He scratched the back of his neck and walked out the door to join the others.

Alone in his office, Karoulis felt the blood pounding in his temple and neck. Fucking animals! he thought. Fucking lasers! Fucking *every*thing!

He closed his eyes then and saw, as he did more and more often, the island with the blue-green water, the sky clear and still, a kid in short pants, and his mother's face.

Chapter 16

Elaine had gotten up to get Barbie off to school and to phone in sick at work. Then she returned to bed, where she had left Mitch sleeping soundly, and curled into his secure contours beneath the warmth of the blankets. For the next hour or so, she drifted in and out of a dreamy sleep, while Mitch slept, unmoving.

The beeping of the V-phone at the bedside roused her. Without pressing the video button, she lifted the receiver to her ear.

"Hello?"

"Hello. Mrs. Helwig? It's Huziak at the station. Is Mitch there?"

"He's still sleeping. Can I take a message?" Mitch was stirring, rolling, listening now with half-open lids.

"If he's there, I think you better wake him for me. It's important."

"He's off today, you know."

"I know. I still need to speak to him."

Without waiting for her to reply, Mitch reached up and took the phone from her hand and held it to his ear. "'Morning. What can I do for you?"

"'Morning, Mitch. Sorry to disturb you like this. Captain's orders." He cleared his throat. "One of our men got shot early this morning, and Karoulis wants a dragnet thrown up around the area where the shooting took place. We're gonna need hundreds, Mitch. Calls are going out now to other adjacent forces and to all off-duty officers to ask for sanctioned help and for volunteer help."

"Volunteer?" The word was out before Mitch could think.

"That's right. The captain is really hopping about this one. He's thrown away the rule book. I think he might have a point. Want to get involved?"

"Tell me more. Who was shot? What happened?"

"Mark Fedwick. Know him?"

"I know who he is. I've met him. Is he alive?"

"Barely. Just barely. He answered an alarm at a computer factory on Wicksteed this morning, went in alone without waiting for a backup, and was cut down. A laser. Three hits in the torso, two in the arms. He's really bad."

Mitch said nothing.

"You still there?"

Mitch took a deep breath. "Yeah. I'm still here."

"We can use you, Mitch."

"I'll be there."

"Thanks, Mitch."

Pressing the button on the receiver, Mitch ended the conversation.

Sitting beside him, Elaine began to rub his back. "I guess that's the end of our glorious day in bed together."

"I have to go."

"I know." She continued to rub his back.

"Bastards. We've got to stop this, you know."

"What can you do?"

"Well, this is something. At least Karoulis is finally sitting up and taking notice."

"He said he wanted volunteers. Will you get paid for going in today?"

"Don't know. I doubt it though. Budget. That's all we ever hear, remember?"

"Are you sure you should be going then?"

He looked at her. "Yes."

She said nothing for a while as he got out of bed and dressed, hauling out his uniform.

"Why didn't he wait for a backup?" she asked. "Why wasn't he more wary?"

Mitch was tucking his shirt into his pants. "It's the odds. They just finally caught up to him."

"What do you mean?"

"Odds always favor that the alarm will be false." He buckled his belt. "Odds favor that the wind rattled a door, that a book fell off a shelf, that an unwitting employee tripped up the system." He buttoned the cuffs on his shirt. "I've seen the statistics. Last year we answered almost a quarter-million alarms in the Metro area. About two thousand of them were valid. Less than one in a hundred. So you see, Fedwick had reason to feel secure when he answered this one, too. Your guard goes down; you become nonchalant. It can be a year or two before you draw a valid alarm, before you randomly pull out the short straw. And then, the last thing you expect is that you're going to be assassinated as you walk through the door. It'd be easy to have a million other things in your head in the middle of the night, to not be paying total attention. A third of all false alarms are attributed to system malfunction, a fifth to human error, the rest to weather and security-alarm testings. It's the whole system. It stinks. Companies with an unacceptable quota of false alarms should simply be cut off. That way we'd shift the odds slightly; that way, more cops would be likely to be anticipating an illegal entry when responding to an alarm."

"I've never understood why you didn't just use police dogs first—send them in to answer an alarm. Let them get killed if there's anyone there crazy enough to kill."

Mitch pulled on his boots and stood up. "They'd tell you 'budget' again. The magic word." A look of wry pain crossed his face. "But it's never that simple. And," he added, "they lie to you. You never get to hear the paranoia that results in the real reason. It's always politics—keeping some pressure group happy. The SPCA maybe. Can you imagine the hue and cry if we said we were going to use dogs the way they used canaries in the coal mines in England? As expendables to warn us of danger?" He shook his head. "The antivivisectionists would be out in force; the humane society. The fucking stoop 'n' scoopers would have a coronary."

"I think you're the one who's going to have the coronary." She got up and kissed him, and he gradually put his arms around her and held her to him tightly. "Go," she said. "Do what you have to do."

Her eyes told him that she understood.

In the hall, he took his duffle bag from its place in the closet, gripping it in a fist that caused the knuckles to turn to snow.

He suspected that he would never find Mario's killer. It was bigger than Mario, bigger than him.

They would all have to pay. He would see to it.

Chapter 17

"Did I ever tell you about Max Rosen?"

Mitch turned and glanced at Mario, who was driving, his left arm resting out the open window of the cruiser.

"Don't think so."

"He was one of my closest friends in high school. He was crazy, though. I think that's why I liked him."

"You mean you had something in common."

Mario gave Mitch a quick, wry, dismissive glance. "Yeah. Both our names begin with 'M.'"

Mitch smiled. "So, what's the story with Max Rosen?"

"Well, he was a drummer in the high school band—you know, percussion."

"I understand a percussion can be serious. Hope he was O.K."

"You dumb ass."

Mitch smiled.

"Anyway, after high school he drifted to Europe and met up with some guy in Italy who played electric organ. Together, they did a few gigs in Greece, then moved to Scandinavia."

"Seen him lately?"

"Naw. That's just it. We swap the odd letter—couple of times a year, maybe. Got one from him yesterday."

"Still in Scandinavia?"

"He's in Greenland."

"Greenland!"

Mario smiled and nodded. "Incredible, eh?"

"Greenland!" Mitch shook his head, trying to decide if he was being put on or not. It didn't seem to be the case. "What the hell does one do in fucking Greenland?"

"He and this other guy answered an ad and ended up as a two-man band in Jakobshavn."

"Where?"

"Do you have to get everything twice?"

"In this case, I think I do."

"Jakobshavn. According to his letter, it's above the Arctic Circle. Says it has three thousand husky dogs and thirty-seven hundred people, mainly Inuit."

"Where does a two-man band play in Jakobshavn? And for whom?"

"Some hotel there."

"You mean people actually go there? Outsiders? Enough to maintain a hotel?" Mitch paused, thinking about it. "Amazing."

"His letter was full of wild stuff. Really interesting."

"How long's he going to stay there? Or does he know?"

"Probably all his life."

Mitch looked perplexed. "Why? What for?"

"He married a local Inuit girl. He's got ties now." Mario was silent for a minute, driving easily. "Something like us."

"I fail to see the similarity."

"We ain't going anywhere. He ain't either."

"But what the hell could you do in Greenland? At least here, you can, you can . . . go to a show, or—"

"Get mugged."

"Or watch TV, go out to a nice restaurant—"

"You can do all that stuff in Jakobshavn."

"C'mon, Mario. You don't really believe that. That's the end of the world up there. The fucking *end!*"

"It's only forty kilometers from North America."

"Yeah. Right. Forty kilometers. If you count Ellesmere Island as part of *any*thing—let alone embellish it by terming it part of North America. It's about as pertinent to North America as . . . as Easter Island is, for Christ's sake."

They were both quiet for a moment. Mitch wasn't sure why he had reacted so passionately. He was rather surprised at himself. He couldn't believe Mario's support of his friend's decision to live in Greenland. It was the last thing he would have expected from the irreverent Italian. Maybe, he thought, they were closer friends than I can understand. Or maybe impending parenthood is playing on his mind, making him take a long, slow look at his surroundings.

"Max Rosen," Mitch said, finally.

Mario didn't respond.

"Jewish?"

Mario nodded. "His parents are having a bird. They raise him up to go to the temple, to take his place in society, and he off and goes to Greenland." He smiled.

Mitch felt he should let Mario talk about it if he wanted, without putting him so much on the defensive. "So," he asked, "what *does* he do in Jakobshavn?"

"He says there are apartment blocks there. And flowers flown from Europe. Even got tequila at the booze counter. And dishes for receiving hockey and soccer games on TV, and stores that sell blue movies on videocassettes." He looked at Mitch briefly. "He can do what we can do, and he can do it safer, *and* he gets to watch the sun after midnight if he wants."

"That's unnatural," Mitch said.

"What is?"

"The sun after midnight. That's weird."

"And fingerprinting seven-year-olds against possible future abductions . . . footprinting infants . . . smuggling dope into the country inside dead birds and crocodile skins—that's natural, eh? That's normal."

"What're you talking about? Dead birds, crocodile skins . . ."

"I heard the guys in Narcotics talking about it last night. Some wildlife preservation group has discovered that the white 'preservative' powder they sometimes find sprinkled on crocodile skins is really cocaine or heroin. The guys who receive 'em just vacuum it off. Same goes for the birds. A shipment of exotic birds comes in from animal dealers in South America. Customs officials aren't too surprised to discover that some of them have died in transit. Now they're discovering the birds have been killed before being shipped out and their bodies stuffed with drugs. Why, Helwig, old boy! We've left old Greenland with mud on its face. How can it ever hope to match the achievements of the civilized world? Eh?''

Mitch was silent again. Finally, he said, ''Do they need cops in Greenland?''

Mario looked at him and chuckled. ''Just to arrest the jerks who shoot more than three deer a year for their pot.'' They drove on for several minutes without speaking. ''You ever think you'd like to move away? Anywhere?''

''No. I like it here.'' He paused. ''Don't you?''

Mario was tugging idly at one end of his bushy moustache. ''Don't know,'' he said. ''Don't know if it's a good place to raise a kid.'' Then he glanced at Mitch. ''Is it?''

Mitch, too, was silent for a moment. Then he said, ''Don't know.''

A red light ahead eased them to a stop. They met one another's eyes, and Mitch said, ''Greenland, eh?''

Mario's dark eyes twinkled in response and his white teeth surfaced in a slow smile. ''Fucking Greenland,'' he said.

Chapter 18

''Captain?''

''What is it, Huziak?''

The sergeant cleared his throat and did everything but hem and haw. Karoulis looked up from his paper-strewn desk, his eyebrows creasing his forehead as he waited.

"Well, uh, it's noon, and I was wondering—as were the others—how long you wanted the dragnet for Fedwick's killer to stay in effect."

Karoulis sat silently.

"I mean, you know, the chances of actually stopping a vehicle with the guy in it—or even knowing it was the guy if you did happen to stop the right vehicle—are, uh, pretty slim."

Karoulis still didn't answer.

"News on both radio and TV is having a field day with it. You know—police overkill, that sort of thing."

Karoulis finally spoke. "Police overkill, my ass."

Huziak looked apologetic. "It's what they're saying."

Karoulis met Huziak's eyes. "Suppose Fedwick was their father, or their son, or their husband. Do you think the jackasses would still scream 'overkill'?" He looked away. "You bet your sweet ass, they wouldn't. Hypocritical bastards. And it's not as if it's costing the taxpayers anything extra. It's only the volunteers that made it possible. So what's the squawk? You tell me—what's the squawk? Eh?"

Huziak shrugged, waiting. Then he turned to leave the office.

"Huziak."

The sergeant turned.

"You're right. Tell the men it's over. Thank them. And give me a list of everyone who volunteered. I'd like to know who was involved, so I can thank them all personally."

"Yes, Captain."

Karoulis stood up and walked over to the row of file cabinets, leaned an elbow on one, and was silent for a minute. Then, without facing Huziak, he asked, "You think the laser is one of the stolen ones from the armory?"

"Don't know, Captain. No way of telling. There were a few kicking around before. Now . . ." He puffed his cheeks and exhaled a steady stream of air, his face showing the strain that had been building.

Kaorulis nodded, his back still to the sergeant. "One other thing," he continued, as Huziak headed once more for the door.

Huziak stopped, waiting.

"How's Fedwick doing?"

"Bad."

"He going to make it?"

"Doesn't look like it. He's tough, though. Doctors say that he should be dead now."

"He ever regain consciousness?"

"No."

Karoulis turned, still leaning on the file cabinet, and stared at Huziak. "What do you think we should do?"

"What do you mean, Captain?"

"It's just a hypothetical question, Sergeant. I mean, what would you do if you were me?"

"You mean about the dragnet?"

"I mean, about everything. About Fedwick, about the laser heist, about ballistics being a dying science. About guys throwing their refrigerators out of apartment windows. About, simply, never catching the guys who do this stuff anymore, unless they're so stupid they're barely alive." He continued to stare at his desk sergeant. "What would you do?"

Huziak shuffled his feet and then met his superior's steady gaze. "I guess, Captain, I'd do what you're doing."

"And what's that, Sergeant? What's that?"

"The best you can."

At 2:20 P.M. Karoulis glanced up to see who was rapping at his office door and saw Peter DeMarco standing there. Karoulis's face twitched with a combination of fear and hope, wondering what news his Homicide detective had for him. He motioned DeMarco in with a wave of his hand.

"Yes?"

"Nothing to do with the Fedwick case, Captain." He eased himself inside the door, obviously waiting to be asked more.

"What is it then, Peter?"

"Three more bodies, Captain."

"Christ. Where? When?"

"They were found this morning. But in all the excitement of the Fedwick shooting, the dragnet and all, I decided to save it for later."

"Small mercies." Karoulis looked grim.

"Two of them are small-time punks—Eddie Stadnyk and Lionel Santos, a.k.a. the Loon. They were both found dead in a service alley north of the Danforth, in the exact same place where we found that guy gutted the other night—you know, Barros."

"Yeah. Yeah. The guy Helwig found. The *exact* same place, you say?"

"Well, exact to within a few feet."

"What's the connection? Can you figure it?"

"We figure Stadnyk probably killed Barros the other night. He had a skinner in his fist when he died—the same type of thing that did the job on Barros. It's being run through the lab right now to see if it'll tell us anything. I'm betting it's the murder weapon."

"How were these guys killed?"

"Laser."

"Jesus. It's getting so I don't have to ask anymore."

"Stadnyk took his in the forehead. Looks like he was lunging at his assailant when he got it. Santos was burned through the heart—much more precise, I'd say."

"You said there were three."

"Yeah. There was another guy about ten meters away—near the street. He'd been cut down, too, by a laser that took him in the chest, near the heart. Name was Sten Doppleman. A known pusher, and a punk in several meanings of the word. You know, eyebrows plucked, blue hair, all spiked. Kind of kid you'd like your daughter to bring home—if it were Halloween. According to his dope sheet, he's a vicious son of a bitch. Actually, they were three of a kind, that way."

"How do you read it all?"

"Well, not sure, naturally. But there is a twist to it all that I wanted to mention to you, Captain."

"I'm listening."

"Two photos are missing from my files. I think someone lifted them."

Karoulis's eyebrows raised, but he said nothing.

DeMarco continued. "One photo was of Barros. The other was of Mario Ciracella."

Karoulis's eyes narrowed as his thoughts filled in gaps. Several pieces slid uncomfortably into place—not giving him a complete picture; rather, just enough of a possible scenario to chill him slightly.

"Mitch Helwig," he muttered.

"Can't say for sure what it means, Captain. But there's something there. Helwig found Barros. And we all know how he almost went over the deep end when he found Ciracella. He hasn't come out of it yet, I don't think."

"I don't think so either."

"And, if we count that punk who was found lasered in the variety store a couple of weeks back, that's a total of four bodies, all lasered—executed almost—on Helwig's usual run." He paused. "What do you think?"

Karoulis bit the inside of his lip and then slowly rubbed the prominent cheekbone under his tired right eye while he thought. His left eye felt just as tired, and his chest sagged visibly.

I feel very old, he thought.

He turned and sat down at his desk. It gave him a bit more time. Finally, he said, "Leave it with me, DeMarco. O.K.?"

The detective nodded. "Whatever you say, Captain." He felt a certain relief at having it handed over to Karoulis. It was certain to be a can of worms, and he didn't really want any part of it. He liked Helwig. Everybody did. But it was more than a little coincidental—anyone could see that. I had to mention it, he rationalized.

Anyway, that's what police captains get all those big bucks for—making these shitty decisions.

DeMarco knew then that he never really wanted to be a captain, no matter how much he occasionally fantasized about the position. Karoulis looks like hell, he thought. Like pure, bloody hell.

"I'll talk to him," Karoulis said.

PART
TWO

Now conscience wakes despair
That slumber'd—wakes the bitter memory
Of what he was, what is, and what must be.
—JOHN MILTON,
Paradise Lost (4.23)

This is the night
That either makes me or fordoes me quite.
—WILLIAM SHAKESPEARE
Othello (5.1.128)

Chapter 19

Herrington Storage was the largest of several nondescript, gray metal warehouses on Commercial Road. The entire area was a remnant of a time long gone—a time when the area of Leaside had been a separate entity, a village in its own right. Now, like virtually every other locale of similar dimensions and proximity, it had been engulfed by metropolitan Toronto, swallowed voraciously into the belly of the whale, where it sat, like a stone, or perhaps a fur ball, resisting total assimilation. The eastern portion of the one-time village consisted of colorless factories, sprawling truck yards, anonymous warehouses—a legacy of the twentieth century, when the area was used as a base for, variously, a World War I vintage airfield; a World War II munitions plant area; and finally, nothing much at all.

Its abandonment by the city's developers and moguls was a curious irony in itself, since it was centrally located and occupied what could only be termed prime real estate. If the city fathers were somewhat myopic regarding its various potentials, the same could not be said of certain other groups. One group in particular had been meticulously acquiring property in the area for years, until now it owned sizable numbers of buildings and assorted types of businesses: from car-wrecking yards to electronic-parts factories, from toy warehouses to upholstery manufacturers. There were buildings—all low-rise—with such vague nomenclatures as Canfab Equipment Supplies, Formex Industrial Products, Jarwick Manufacturing Co., and Standard Simulations, a Division of Feltran International. What exactly they produced or traded in was not widely known; nor were many curious. Many of the businesses were completely legitimate—on the surface—and so many others surrounding them were *truly* legitimate that they managed to become suitably unobtrusive merely by geographical propinquity. And they did nothing on purpose to draw attention to themselves.

One of the most unassuming was the largest: Herrington Storage. Overtly, its business consisted of storing products, supplies, and materials used or voided by kindred surrounding businesses. So enormous was it that it covered most of an extensive city block, fronting on two parallel streets. At any given time, there were usually a minimum of a half-dozen tractor-trailers docked at various bays, either on the streets themselves or at the bays inside the link-wire fencing topped with barbed wire; they were, alternately, being loaded or unloaded. Seldom, to any alert eye, was there no activity at all. Similarly, the precise nature of the activities was never evident either. The building existed somewhat as a beehive exists—with everyone assuming that what goes on inside is what goes on in every beehive; namely, busy-busy activity of a humdrum sort. Perhaps the parallel could be extended further: eventually, people learn to leave beehives alone in order to avoid being stung, once they see or hear of the effects. People seek comfort and pleasure, not nuisance and pain. Live and let live. For the most part.

Arcangelo Scopellini drove his executive silver Cadillac coupe, with the spiked wheel covers, up to the gatehouse, where the security guard was passing the time with a paperback novel. As he let the tinted automatic window slip slowly down so that he might be identified, he removed his dark glasses as he always did.

"'Morning, John.''

"Good morning, Mr. Scopellini. How are you today?''

"Fine, thank you.''

The guard pressed a button and the steel bars slid out of their berth in the opposite wall. The tinted window slid back up and Arcangelo Scopellini put his dark glasses back onto his tanned, sculptured face, eased his foot off the brake, and glided into the wide yard, heading for his personal parking space.

Before opening the car door, he checked his maroon silk tie in the rear-view mirror, ran a finger along his tapered moustache, and adjusted his dark glasses on the Roman bridge of his nose. Satisfied, he stepped out, his leather briefcase in hand, and strode across the asphalted yard and through the closest gaping truck entranceway, nodding occasionally as he was intermittently recognized. Most of those whom he encountered had the good sense to affect disinterest in him, no matter how curious or awed they might in fact be; only a few less prudent found themselves openly turning and gazing in fascination as the Archangel melted by.

Fifty some years ago, when he was born, to immigrant factory workers in Montreal, his mother could have had no inkling of how her chosen name would be transmuted so venerably. His two brothers had been Michael and Gabriel, but both perished mere hours after their premature births. When the third child was born—also a son, and also prematurely—she pulled out all the stops, not naming him Raphael as she had planned, but calling him, in a manner, after all three, as her part of a silent, desperate bargain with heaven, the Blessed Virgin, and the angels themselves. In her mind, it had worked, for this son had lived, and indeed prospered, for did he not send enough money home every month, even to this day, to more than fill her needs as an aging widow?

God had indeed been kind, and in response she had sent the Archangel into the world.

And the Archangel had spread his ominous wings and shadow over the land, bringing an almost preternatural gift to an ever-darkening vision of his place in the world. As the mouth of the warehouse that was Herrington Storage swallowed him into its maw, he felt at ease; this great, hulking artifice of a cavern was a suitable habitat for him, and unfailingly, he responded to the stale, dry air of its interior by feeling as though, somehow, he had glided back home. This was his lair. It suited him, as open air or brightly lit office buildings never could.

His world.

He strode up the metal stairs and along the see-through catwalk that rimmed the warehouse's interior. For two more minutes he maintained the same, steady gait, arriving finally at the steel door that was his destination, comforted by the knowledge that he had been video- and motion-monitored for the last minute. He opened the combination lock on the door, inserted his key to turn the final tumblers, and went into his private office.

It was as he had left it the previous evening. It was always as he left it the previous evening. No one else had access to this particular room in the warehouse; this was the Archangel's sanctum. The room, about six meters by six meters, was sparsely but sensibly furnished: a desk, two chairs, a sofa, a wall of shelves, filled with rows of videotapes and software and irregular piles of paper, a wall of file cabinets; the top of the desk was cluttered with more paper and an array of electronic communication equipment. The ashtray on the desk was full and, as was his habit, the first thing he did was dump the contents into the wastebasket so that he could commence another day of filling it. A clean start, as it were.

This done, he flipped the plastic lid from one of the consoles on his desktop and pressed a button. Opposite him, the metal plate covering the room's lone window slid up, and he gazed down onto the acres of crates and forklifts and gray figures moving about below, and lit his first dark cheroot of the day. The smoke drifted in a luxuriant tendril, dissipating into the air circulation system grilles in the ceiling.

It was, he thought, a fine thing to have such privacy and quiet and security in which to work.

And such control.

He let the start of the day flow slowly over him, and let the smoke flow sensuously from his nostrils in response. There was much to think about, as always. And there was his mother's birthday next week. He wondered if he would be able to get away for it, and decided to double his efforts to try, having missed the last two. Something always came up; it was, he reflected, the nature of the business.

Finally, he turned his attention to the small red light on the intercom, which had been glowing since he entered the room, and pressed yet another button in the plastic desk console. Immediately, the face of one of the secretaries in the office at the building's front entrance blossomed onto his screen.

"A message for me?"

"Yes, Mr. Scopellini. Mr. Purdon, Mr. Otis, and Mr. Osika have been waiting for you to arrive. May they see you?"

The Archangel was pleased that they had acted so promptly. "Send them up." Clicking off the transmission, he sat down and contented himself with arranging pens, papers, and his ashtray on his desk. Then, in preparation for the arrival of the three men, he extracted his Barking Dog from a desk drawer, spent a minute attaching it through the front of his shirt, and then let it hang openly from the chest pocket of his jacket, in full view; in a situation like this, it often simplified matters if everyone knew of its presence in advance. It saved much time.

Rising from the swivel chair, he went to the window, spotted the trio on the warehouse floor in the distance, and followed their progress across the vast gray expanse, up the catwalk steps and along the metal walkway, noting how Osika was always positioned between Purdon and Otis.

These things, he knew, had to be done. There could be no exceptions.

He had liked Thomas Osika.

Opening the door, he gestured for them to enter. With the proper degree of deference—or perhaps even fear—they obliged, standing in the center of the room while he closed the door and walked back to his swivel chair, where he seated himself with a sigh.

The Barking Dog glittered against his navy blue suit, and he tapped it slowly and obviously. "You understand, gentlemen?"

They nodded.

"Good. It makes things so much simpler."

They remained standing. He let them stand for an unnecessary minute longer, orchestrating the effects, fine-tuning his estimable presence in their midst.

"Daniel, Charles, be seated. Thomas, remain standing." Otis and Purdon turned and sat on the sofa, while Osika maintained his place at the center of the exhibit. The Archangel eyed him thoughtfully. No expression, he thought. It's true what they say about Orientals: they can be inscrutable. One does not read them the way one reads men like Otis and Purdon. Or the way one can read me, even.

But the Dog, he knew, could read everything.

Its huge eye stared unblinkingly.

The Archangel sighed dramatically once again, shaking his head with a world-weariness that was both postured and sincere. "Stupid, Thomas. Very stupid."

Osika remained staunch. Neither of the other two dared to move.

"I shall recount the events as I know them, Thomas. When I have finished, you are free to correct them or to refute them, so that the truth can be aired. Is that all right?"

Osika spoke his first words. "Yes, sir." The Archangel thought he detected the beginnings of a perspiration moustache on the young Oriental's upper lip.

The Barking Dog absorbed everything.

"On Monday, the twenty-second, you and three others used your access to the warehouse to borrow two items that you then used for your personal gain, without authorization or approval from me or anyone else. On or about midnight, you removed a truck with a mobile crane and one of our most recent acquisitions, a seventy-centimeter laser cannon, and went to the Rosedale home of Justice Gordon McKnight. Mr. McKnight, as I understand it, owns a Porsche XK9000, imported as a special bauble for his own private pleasure, at a cost of over one hundred thousand dollars. To ensure its safety, he parks it in a locked stone garage behind a three-meter-high wall on his property. It appears that you and your friends used the crane to lower yourselves over the wall and onto the garage roof, where you then proceeded to use the laser cannon to slice the roof into sections which you attached to the crane and lowered to the ground until the automobile was completely exposed. You then attached the crane to the vehicle itself and hoisted it out of the garage and lowered it onto the truck.'' He paused. Neither Otis nor Purdon had so much as moved a muscle. ''Am I correct so far?''

The Oriental's eyes betrayed nothing. ''Yes,'' he said.

It was the truth. Pleased at the smoothness of the potentially sticky situation, the Archangel continued.

''Where is the vehicle now?''

''It is gone.''

The Archangel nodded. ''I was afraid as much.'' He let a moment of silence intervene as he thought, then he asked: ''Gone where?''

Osika licked his lips. ''A wrecker. A chop-shop. For parts.''

''How much did you get?''

Osika let his glance fall onto the Barking Dog before deciding on the answer he would give. ''Thirty thousand,'' he said.

''About thirty cents on the dollar,'' the Archangel muttered, more to himself than to the others. ''Are you sure it was chopped for parts?''

''No, I'm not sure. He may have lied. He may have sold it intact. I don't know.''

''But you can't get it back?''

''No.''

''Could you buy it back from him?''

''No.''

''Why?''

''He wouldn't sell it. It's too rare.''

There was a tremor of frostbite in the Archangel's side. It was not the whole truth.

''I'll ask again—but only once. Why?''

Osika looked shaken, for the first time, that even this slight nuance on the truth had been apprehended. His voice became lower as his defenses disappeared altogether. "I don't have the money anymore. I split half of it with the others. My share is gone."

"Gone where?"

The Oriental felt the web wind tighter about him, squeezing. He became more stoic in response. "Debts. I had to pay debts."

"You were getting a good salary from us, Thomas. I'm sorry to hear you were not able to live within your means. It's the sign of a man who lacks vision."

The room was silent.

"You lack vision, Thomas. You do not see the future as it should unfold. It is a grievous shortcoming. An unaffordable one." He mused a moment, then decided to explain further. "Gordon McKnight called me personally. He is a man we do much business with. He is very angry. The car was his personal toy, a small vanity that he indulged in with childlike joy."

Osika tried to explain. "I didn't know who he was. I just knew he was a wealthy man who owned a rare car. I did not wish to cause you trouble."

"But you have caused me trouble, Thomas. And, you overstepped your bounds vastly by employing our equipment on such a venal and petty expedition. Personal profit, personal debts . . ." He shook his head. "You disappoint me. I thought you understood. In fact, I'm sure you did understand—and still do. You merely gambled and lost, is that not it? The same way you ended up with debts in the first place? Many bad habits and character flaws tumble one upon the other, the result being a man without vision—a man who will cause, at best, small interruptions within an organization such as ours, or at worst, large, unnecessary moments of internal chaos."

Still, no one spoke but the Archangel. He asked, finally, "Were you drinking, Thomas?"

When he did not respond, the Archangel prompted him. "Answer, Thomas. The truth."

The voice was weak. "Yes."

Bridging his hands before him, the Archangel nodded. On the sofa, both Otis and Purdon remained frozen, knowing with a sense of vision themselves where all this was heading, glad only that they were not in Osika's place, on the mat in front of the Archangel and the Barking Dog. The smoke from the dark cheroot gave the room a bizarre, churchly atmosphere, smelling as it did of some ancient frankincense.

Turning his attention to the men on the sofa, the Archangel asked, "The other three . . . they've been taken care of?"

Otis took the initiative. "Yes, sir."

Osika's cheek twitched involuntarily as he heard this.

"Fine." He looked back at Osika. "You overstepped yourself, Thomas. There is no turning back now. You have chosen your path, fraught as it was with risk, knowing full well the possible consequences. Your vision failed you in that you could not see yourself stumbling, being exposed. One must always allow for such a possibility, always see it in the cards as a possible hand that may be dealt." He shrugged. "It is the way it ends. Someone always scrapes up the pot in the center of the table. If it is not you, then you should be prepared to pay the price. Only then can one gamble with acumen. You, Thomas, gambled stupidly. And now, we all pay, in one way or another: time, inconvenience, money, embarrassment—for your blunder. And you," he added, as a finale, "pay with your life."

The perspiration on Osika's upper lip had spread to become the perspiration on his brow as well. To his credit, though, thought the Archangel, he did not quaver, did not beg.

Inscrutable to the last. You had to give them credit. They knew how to face the end.

"Daniel, Charles . . ."

The two men rose to their feet.

"Take Mr. Osika out now."

The Japanese man's eyes became colorless as they bored into the eyes of the man seated in the swivel chair, who had just acted as his judge. Then they became blank, and his jaw clenched as he was led from the room. The door clicked behind them, and exhaling smoke lazily from his nostrils, the Archangel stood and strode to the window. He stood there, watching, until the three men below disappeared through a door, headed for the basement of the warehouse.

The day had started.

Now, he thought, to business. He made a few notes on a piece of paper: new Porsche XK9000 for Justice Gordon McKnight; repairs to garage; quick disposal of eleven thousand .38 caliber handguns.

He paused, looked up from his paper. They had to be moved quickly, and in bulk, he knew, before they devalued to insignificance with the spate of lasers coming onto the market. It was one reason he had been so upset that Osika had taken an unauthorized laser cannon out on his own petty heist. They were being kept off the market until the handguns had been moved. If it became commonly known that they had over six thousand new lasers in stock, the bottom would fall out of the .38 market. Not that they couldn't afford it, he knew. It just created an unnecessary headache, and he had had enough of that for today.

Besides—it was bad business. It showed, he thought, a lack of vision.

When he left the warehouse yard at 6 P.M. that evening, Arcangelo Scopellini failed to notice the lone man sitting in a car parked halfway down the street. And even if he had seen the man—or, in fact, driven right past and looked in at him—he still would not have thought anything, for the Archangel had no reason to recognize Mitch Helwig.

The Archangel was tired, and he still had to find a florist on the way home and place an order for his traditional dried-flower arrangement, something he never forgot for his mother's birthday.

Chapter 20

In the cafeteria of the Nishiyama building on Markham Road, Elaine Helwig sipped her morning coffee and thumbed through a copy of the *Sun*. The headline reported the major item of the day: "Metro Officer Loses Valiant Fight For Life."

Mark Fedwick had not made it.

On page two, the feature story was entitled "Death Revives Issue of Restoring Capital Punishment for Murder."

For the life of her, Elaine could never fathom why capital punishment was such a contentious issue. Every Canadian referendum on the subject for the last twenty-five years had spelled out loudly and clearly that the people themselves wanted capital punishment as an option. The States had reinstated it in all but five of the fifty states to date. But Canada seemed bound by the same political arrogance that was reflected in Great Britain—even though the people always called for its legislative reinstatement, the politicians stonewalled it, acting on their own personal sense of political fragility. None of them wanted to be identified as the one who had been responsible. Elaine was constantly amazed that they read the situation in that way, for it seemed to her that the public was just waiting to find a champion for their beliefs and desires, and that the one who was finally responsible for its return would, in fact, garner many, many votes. She wondered who they thought they were shielding themselves from.

Politics, by its very nature, she knew, could not deal with truths or with precise answers or decisions. If you asked anyone at Nishiyama, right here where she worked, what they thought should be done about a specific issue, they'd tell you. Ask them, for example, what should be done about, say, prostitution, and at least they'd come right out and give their opinion. But ask a politician, and you'd hear, "There are three ways that one can see the situation . . ." and then you'd be forced to sit through the tedium of listening to the old fart proselytize for five minutes without ever telling you what *he* thought of it all, since all he was ever really thinking about was the effect his words would have on various pressure groups that control blocs of votes. *How will the feminists read it? How will the Catholics see it?* Never mind that he personally felt it should be modeled after the legalized setup existing in sixteen States below the border, with all the controls that such a situation entails. He could never say that. It might be politically imprudent.

Fear.

So he said nothing. But took five minutes to do it. It was an old story. Nothing new.

Elaine flipped the page.

But it had got her wondering. Why, she mused, are we so afraid to try anything new to stem the tide? What makes us think that what we've done for a few hundred years is some sort of eternal verity?

She remembered reading an article somewhere that proposed how violent criminals should all be sterilized and kept in a wilderness camp in the North. Bars would not be necessary, it suggested, for escape would automatically entail death by exposure and starvation rather quickly. Guards would consist of well-armed, frequently rotated members of the armed forces, with orders to shoot to kill at the first sign of violence or insurrection. The camp would promote hard physical work, raising one's own food, repair and upkeep of one's dwelling, production of one's own clothing and furniture. Women prisoners could sleep in camps some distance from the men's quarters, and sexual visitations could be structured into the routines.

When she had tried to discuss it with a few of the people at work, she had been hooted down as some form of fanatic, and the jokes and innuendos had begun to fly. Shyly, she had backed down, never mentioning that it seemed perfectly sensible to her. And still, no one had shown her why it might be unfeasible. It was merely dismissed as some sort of madman's vision, allied with the atrocities of Hitler and Stalin, although any reading of either history or philosophy would quickly put the boot to such uninformed scoffing.

No one seemed to want to admit that some people are genuine dangers to society and that there can be no logical reason for preserving them. Our Christian ethic, the New Testament: turn the other cheek, punishment is the Lord's; not so in the times of the Old Testament: an eye for an eye . . .

And now, perhaps times had changed again. Who was to say they had not? Who was to define what constituted terms of war, when even the religionists dropped the reins?

Certainly not the politicians.

Elaine felt the old urge for a cigarette that crept up occasionally, fought it, conquered it. Too much happening lately, she thought. First Mario, and now Mitch . . . And in the middle of it, I'm supposed to just keep going to work and coming home as though nothing's happening. Off to Nishiyama Computerworks five days a week, after getting Barbie off to school. Thank God, she thought, for Mrs. Chan, and her help after school and evenings with Barbie. I don't know how I'd manage.

And Jan . . . Let's not forget Jan, she thought. She needs me, too. Everybody needs me. What about *me?* What about *my* life? What is my life, anyway?

Checking her watch, she saw that she still had ten minutes before going upstairs to the office. She flipped more pages, her eyes restless and weary. The coffee was cold now.

On page thirty-six, another item caught her eye: "Wives Work for Cash—Not 'Self-Fulfillment,' Study Says." It read:

The sheer need for money—not "self-fulfillment"—is the main reason wives exist in the workforce in record numbers, a national study indicates.

"The notion has been put out that wives are working to fulfill their own sense of enlightened equality," said Peter Elford, a Statistics Canada official who conducted the study. "But the basic reason appears to be the drive to maintain their family's income, in the face of hardship caused by inflation and husbands' falling real incomes," Elford said in an interview. "During the '90s, the wife's contribution increasingly sustained the family."

The major findings:

Ten years ago, twelve percent of all husband-wife families relied exclusively on the husband's income. By 1998, that rate had dropped to just seven percent.

From 1995 to 1998, husbands' average incomes actually dropped $360 in 1998 dollars, while wives' average incomes rose $270.

Elford is worried about the possible social impact of his findings, especially at the start of the next decade—the onset of the bi-millenium. "The workforce can't continue to add people like it did in the '80s, before the recession hit in full force," he said. That means the trend toward more two-income families may stop or possibly even be reversed, especially in the light of technology that is cutting down on clerical and service jobs, which traditionally are held by women, Elford suggested. A litany of economic woes during the past decade—including rising mortgage and consumer loan rates, and higher home-heating costs and property taxes—placed increased economic pressures on families.

Strains on the family caused by these changes have not yet been examined, Elford said. Early work on the subject pointed to greater influence by wives in family decisions, as their earnings increased. But Elford wants more thorough study of the psychological effects on family role definitions and tensions generated by shifts in family power and influence. "What is at stake," he said, "is the economic health of the Canadian family and the potential need for new family policies."

Elaine looked up, pursing her lips. She thought about the money that was missing from their joint savings, thought about the sacrifices that they both made, both she and Mitch, to make it all work, and wondered what the truth was in her own situation. Mitch was not a politician. He would tell her. If she asked him. If she asked him.

When she asked him.

Elaine Helwig had been doing office and secretarial work for five years at Nishiyama, but it was only since the spring that she had been doing demonstrations. When Jan Prudhomme had asked for time off in the wake of her marital separation—a combination of domestic and personal crises that had sent her to the edge of nervous breakdown—Donald Barbour, Elaine's boss, had asked her if she would step in and help out until things balanced out once more. Jan was her friend, too. She had been as upset as anyone could be who was not directly involved. Of course she had offered to help, especially if it meant that Jan would not be let go permanently, and it was understood that she was only stop-gapping until Jan could return to her job.

What she had not anticipated was how much she would enjoy her new position; the other thing that had taken her aback somewhat was the bond that had grown between herself and Donald Barbour as a result of working together on common projects. The fact was that she spent more time with him than she did with almost any other human being—including her family.

Mitch's shift work, Barbie's growing independence . . .

She felt herself changing, too. Nothing stayed the same. Nothing stood still long enough to take root in any substantial way.

Mostly, it scared her.

Sometimes though, she seized it, welcoming the risk, because risk was one of the few things that she knew could make life worth living.

Passion and risk.

Her job. Donald Barbour. Jan Prudhomme.

Mario Ciracella. Mitch. Barbie.

Her marriage.

Passion and risk.

With five minutes to go before nine o'clock, she tossed the newspaper into the wastebasket and headed toward the elevator, ready to start another day.

But it didn't feel like just another day. It felt different, and she wasn't sure why.

Chapter 21

When the executive silver Cadillac with the spiked wheel covers and the tinted windows turned off Eglinton and began to round the cloverleaf-turn onto the Don Valley Parkway, Mitch discreetly dropped back three car lengths, letting other vehicles slide between them as a shifting, random curtain. For about five minutes they cruised north. The Cadillac, Mitch noted, never changed lanes, always remaining in the inside one, letting faster, or merely more restless, cars glide by. In a vast, undulating river of homeward-bound commuters, it moved like an ocean liner, secure and certain in its position and progress.

At York Mills Road, it eased into the exit lane, veering east, joining the flow once again in the inside lane. Without missing a beat, Mitch followed. They continued on like this for ten minutes; then the Cadillac pulled into a small plaza and slowed, searching out a parking spot. Mitch took the cue, sliding his own aging vehicle into the same lot, hanging well back. He satisfied himself with a parking space off in a far corner, from where he could watch unobserved.

It wasn't really necessary, Mitch knew, to trail this man this way. He had merely become curious. For three days now he had performed his own private stakeout of Herrington, for three days watched the punctual arrival and departure of the tanned, moustached man in the silver Cadillac, and for three days he had known that he was watching Arcangelo Scopellini—the Archangel of note—perform his daily routines in an unassuming and inconspicuous manner. A check of the license number of the silver vehicle had given him a start, and coaxing the names of shareholders of Herrington from the computer had pushed him down the path. It was beginning to fall into place. Mitch even knew where he lived, and his cruise up the Don Valley Parkway confirmed that he was headed home.

Mitch just wanted to see for himself. He wanted to get more of a feel for the man who soared between heaven and hell, arranging the world in the manner that suited him best.

He watched as the Archangel got out of his car, adjusted his dark glasses on his nose, and then entered a small florist shop. Five minutes later, he reappeared, got back in his car, and left the plaza.

Again, Mitch followed.

And when the great silver vehicle turned and glided down a side street, when it slowed and maneuvered into the driveway of a sprawling, luxurious two-story house worth at least one and a half million dollars, Mitch coasted by without flinching, like a hawk riding a high night wind, circling, circling, familiarizing himself with the air currents on which he was silently soaring.

In one way or another, they had all killed Mario.

They would all pay, he thought.

All.

Chapter 22

At four-thirty, Elaine Helwig and Donald Barbour were heading back to Nishiyama in his company Oldsmobile, weary but satisfied from a lengthy day at Safeco Insurance in Mississauga, where they had been demonstrating a new line of both software and hardware. He eased to a red light on the Lakeshore.

She glanced at him. "Think they'll buy?"

"Yes," he said. "I think so. Eventually." He ran his left hand across the five o'clock shadow on his cheek as he pondered it. "This is a strange business, this. With companies like that, the primary thing to accomplish is to convince them that all their competition has already opted for new equipment. Got to make them believe that they'll lose an edge if they fail to keep up." He shrugged. "Paranoia being what it is in this world, it's never as hard as it should be. People convince themselves that they're falling behind."

Elaine paused before commenting. "Well, aren't they?"

He turned to look at her, found himself smiling at the smile she was offering him, found himself glad, as always, that she was with him.

The light turned green.

"You know," he said, "that they'll buy—if they buy at all—because of the hots that supervisor, Norton, had for you."

"Don't be silly."

"Who's being silly? A blind man could see it. He gave off palpable waves of desire. Those closest to him—and you—at lunch were cascaded in a fine mist of seething, corporate lust."

She giggled. "You're ridiculous."

"Yeah. Sure. Right. Ridiculous."

"It was my sheer professionalism." She slid him a mocking glance.

Now it was his turn to shrug, and to continue smiling. "Want me to drop you off at home? Or want to go back to the office? Or . . . want to go somewhere and have a bite to eat?"

Don Barbour had asked Elaine to have dinner with him on a variety of occasions, and each time had received the same thank-you-but-no-thank-you. He liked her a lot, and she felt the same way toward him—or so he thought. How could anyone ever be certain of these things, especially in the fencing stages? he wondered. She was, in his eyes, a classy, attractive woman. He wasn't positive what the state of her marriage was, but he had sensed for some time now that it was in that gray range of most marriages he knew: somewhere between acceptable and tense. Much like my own, he thought. One does not, he reflected, arrive at forty-four years of age, with a seventeen-year marriage and two teenagers in tow, without a deep and perceptive understanding of how most of the world's domestic lives are unfolding. Nor does one arrive at this point, he knew, without some curiosity regarding just who and what else may be out there. It was the rare relationship he had known that managed to encompass a universe for the two participants, a universe that excluded the complexities of other relationships. Donald Barbour did not consider himself a man who chased women. In fact, he did not. But, on occasion, things happened. Things that he did not seek out. Things that were a normal part of everyday life in the business world. And you sometimes met people. People you liked.

People like Elaine Helwig.

So he had graciously, and even admiringly, accepted her refusals to join him for dinner. He wasn't sure what he wanted from such a get-together. He just felt certain that it would be pleasant. And that had been enough.

"I think I'd like that," she said. "Let's get a bite to eat somewhere. I'll call home and see if I can get Mrs. Chan to stay with Barbie till I get back.''

Don raised one eyebrow in pleasant surprise. ''Great. Anyplace in mind?''

''Nope. You pick it.''

''I know a nice spot for some Italian food. How's that sound?''

''Sounds perfect. Can you stop at a V-booth first chance you get?''

''Sure.''

''The sooner I get Mrs. Chan, the better. We shouldn't start making plans that aren't going to happen. She's a vital part of this culinary departure, I hope you realize.''

''Of course she is. Where would any of us be without Mrs. Chan?''

''Exactly. Where?''

They both chuckled. Elaine felt a tiny rush of adrenaline. Passion and risk, she thought. Where have you been for so long?

And what am I doing?

Seated across the table from Don Barbour, Elaine saw a good-looking man with solid, middle-class WASP features. He was the firmly entrenched stereotype of the successful businessman—in many ways, everything that Mitch was not, nor would ever want to be, she reflected. Ruggedly handsome, his moustache was full and black, in contrast to his hair, which had begun to salt-and-pepper. The eyes were blue, the skin tanned, the crow's feet at the corners of the piercing eyes indicative of what was for her the proper level of experience and maturity. He was a sexy and desirable man.

She felt like a schoolgirl on a date. She also felt the rush of quiet excitement that accompanied the secret, the forbidden. Mitch worked till midnight. Mrs. Chan was at her place. Don seemed unconcerned about accounting for himself to anyone, and this made Elaine wonder idly about his relationship with his wife. Was working late at the office a regular occurrence?

As if reading her mind, he said, ''I phoned home about three.

Said I was going to eat at a restaurant, then meet a client." He paused. "I was, too." Then he smiled. "And I'm doing it, aren't I?"

"Am I a client?"

"Is this a restaurant?"

"A client can be many things."

"There are many types of restaurants."

"A client can be a customer, a personal follower . . ."

"There are Italian restaurants, German, French . . ."

"In ancient Rome, a client was a poor or humble person who depended on a noble or wealthy man for assistance."

"Japanese, Chinese . . ." He trailed away. He glanced at her sharply. "Did you say you were poor and humble?"

"No. Nor did I say you were noble or wealthy. That's why we get along so well. We listen to one another and care."

They both smiled.

"So we're finally having dinner together," he said.

"That's right. What can it mean?" she asked coyly.

"It could mean we're both hungry. That we both deserve a nice meal that someone else cooks for us. Especially you."

"Why me?"

"Because, I must admit, I wouldn't be cooking my meal anyway."

"Do you ever cook?"

"Not often. I'm not home in time. You should know about that. Besides, Ruth is better at it than I am. We're both happy with our roles. It's hardly what one could call an imposition. I do what I do, and she does what she does. We both pull our weight. In a lot of ways, she's got a much better deal."

"How's that?"

"She doesn't have to watch guys like that Norton today make a fool of himself."

"Hey! Wait a minute! You said he had the hots for me. Since when does that make him a fool?"

"He was too obvious."

"Ah! You think the drool gave him away."

He shook his head. "That, and when he accidentally swallowed his pencil when you touched his hand while laughing at his joke about the Japanese camera that went 'crick.'"

"I didn't laugh!"

"You smiled too obligingly."

"You can't have it both ways. You want him to buy . . ." She shrugged innocently.

He nodded, beaten.

She watched his blue eyes twinkle, feeling herself drawn down into a vortex of illusion and distraction. Not to have to make dinner was a start. To be out like this, treated like a very special somebody was yet another vital part of it. Escape from Mitch, and whatever it was that was haunting Mitch, was more of it. And some assertion and defiance were mixed in, too. It was everything, blending, roiling, coming apart, separating into unidentifiable fragments that left her curious, daring, and vulnerable. Turning to Don was a natural consequence, she knew. It made sense, in a way that turning to Jan Prudhomme could not at this point. She needed masculine company, masculine approval, masculine understanding of herself—things she was not currently getting from Mitch—things she had not gotten for a long time.

She thought of the missing money. Their money.

"I'd like some wine," she found herself saying.

He let his eyes roam over her face. He saw a mature, attractive woman, a lovely lady, light-years distanced from the fluffy-headed blonds so many of his business acquaintances took up with, much to his embarrassment. This was a lady a man would want to be seen in public with—not just somebody to take to bed for a diversion. We make an attractive pair, he thought proudly.

"An excellent idea," he said. *"In vino veritas."*

"Is it possible to find truth in a ten-dollar bottle of Chianti?"

"It's possible to find it in a four-dollar bottle of gin."

"All of it?"

"Whoever finds all of it?"

"Whoever looks for all of it?"

"Those ancient Romans you were talking about, maybe. Nobody else that I know of. Who wants to know the truth? Most of us are satisfied with pleasure, with the moment. Aren't you?" He reached across the red-and-white checked tablecloth, careful to avoid the slim, flickering white candlestick that let shadows dance enchantingly about them, and took her soft hand in his.

She looked down at the hand engulfing hers, understanding the gesture fully. The small shadows shifted and jumped on their joined flesh. Before closing her hand with his, she looked up into his eyes. "Have you ever read Plato?"

He frowned, puzzled. "I thought we were delving into Roman history."

"Let's diversify. Let's toss in a Greek here or there."

He sensed that she had not yet made a decision about their own future from the limpness of her hand in his, so he went along with her tentatively. "Years ago. More years than I care to think about, actually. When I was an undergraduate. We all read *The Republic*. Had to. Why?"

"Then you've read the *Parable of the Cave?*"

"Have I?"

"If you actually read the assigned book. Did you?"

"Um, let's see. Mmm, yes, that particular one I did read. It was Aristotle's *Ethics* I faked my way through. What did you fake your way through?"

"Most dates when I was a teenager. Anyway, back to the *Parable of the Cave . . .*"

"I read every issue of *People* magazine, from 1977 to 1997. How's that for educated?"

"Awesome."

"Ask me about Mick Jagger's third marriage. I know everything."

She dropped her eyes.

"I'm sorry. You wanted to tell me something."

She shrugged. "It seemed to fit."

"Fit what, Elaine? Tell me. I didn't mean to be so flip that something important would get lost."

She looked back up at him. "In the *Parable,* we're all in the Cave, staring at shadows flickering on the wall of the Cave, with our backs to the light that's casting the shadows. We mistake the shadows for what is Real. We never get out of the Cave."

The slim, pale taper shimmered, its wavering shadow sliding and jumping across the skin of their joined hands and wrists. They both saw it.

"I'm just trying to find out what's real, what's true. Can you understand?" It was her last, imploring stand.

The waiter arrived.

His hand tightened on hers. "Yes," he said. "I think so."

It was acceptable, she decided, this conjunction they had arrived at. She knew she had been staring at shadows on the wall for far too long. She had to look in a different direction, follow whatever leads were provided for her, take a chance.

She had to. And she understood this in a way that was impossible to fully articulate.

They ordered wine.

Chapter 23

When Mitch checked in at the station at noon, Huziak stopped him with a gentle touch on his arm as he passed.

"Captain wants to see you."

Mitch let about five seconds tick by before answering. "What for?"

Huziak shrugged. "Don't know."

"Okay. Thanks."

Huziak nodded.

Mitch felt Huziak's eyes burrowing between his shoulder blades as he headed for Karoulis's office, amid the controlled din and clamor of the shift changeover.

He rapped softly and evenly on the captain's door.

"Come in!"

Mitch pushed the door open and stepped into the room. "You wanted to see me, Captain?"

He thought he saw a pained shadow cross Karoulis's face fleetingly, then disappear. "Yes, Mitch. Come in, please."

Mitch stepped in and closed the door behind him. He remained standing. Karoulis placed his hands on the top of his desk and pushed himself up and out of his seat, sighing, eventually ambling around to the open area of the office where Mitch was standing.

Mitch waited.

Karoulis gazed into his eyes. Mitch stared back, unwaveringly. There was, Mitch sensed, a moment of real contact, just for a second, as they understood and tried to appreciate each other. There was no fencing. It was a standoff: two warriors, veterans, appraising, separating and weighing the disparate elements of respect, admiration, fear, hatred, envy. Men did this with one another, he had always felt, in a way that women did not. It was almost atavistic; tribes could be at stake.

Without taking his eyes from Mitch's, Karoulis slowly held out his right hand, awaiting Mitch's clasp. Mitch's eyes flickered questioningly to the hand, trying to assimilate the gesture. He still couldn't put it all together.

"Thanks, Mitch."

Mitch was silent, watching, listening. Karoulis continued to watch and study his face.

"What for, Captain?"

"For volunteering to help with the Fedwick dragnet. I'm trying to see everyone involved, and thank them personally." His hand was still frozen in midair.

Mitch glanced down at it, then back at the captain's face. He reached out and clasped the hand, squeezing it firmly.

"The fact that Fedwick didn't make it doesn't alter what you and the others did. The fact that we haven't caught the killer, or that the dragnet did not actually snare him, in no way diminishes your commitment and effort."

Mitch nodded. "You don't have to thank me, Captain. I think what you did took a lot of guts. I think it was the right thing to do." He paused. "I know it was the right thing to do."

"I appreciate your words, Mitch. They help."

Their hands parted. Karoulis moved a meter or so laterally out of Mitch's "body space," turned, and faced him again, studying him intently.

"What do you think, Mitch? Have we moved into a time when we need new attitudes toward crime, toward how we should be doing our job?" He was probing, delicately, casually. Mitch sensed his own protective barriers tingle to alertness.

"I told you—I think you did the right thing. It was new. Nobody'd ever done it before. Did it work? I don't know. It didn't *not* work. Nothing was lost by it. If anything, it unified us, made us feel as though someone cared."

"The press didn't like it."

Mitch let an unsavory tone slide into his words. "The press didn't get shot. The press is a bunch of self-appointed, overly theoretical dabblers in rhetoric. They create controversy to sell newspapers. I wouldn't put too much stock in their opinions, Captain."

Karoulis was staring at him intently. "Who would you listen to, then, Mitch?"

Mitch stared back at him. "You have to listen to yourself, Captain. You have to go inside yourself, and see what's there. You have to be willing to take a chance to do what you know is right."

Karoulis leaned against the front of his desk pensively. Neither man spoke for a moment. "What if you're wrong? What if you make a mistake?"

"You didn't make a mistake."

"The union's still going to take me to task."

"Maybe you made a political mistake. That's not even on the same board as a moral mistake. They're different animals."

"Suppose someone on the dragnet had gotten killed, too?"

"They volunteered. I volunteered."

"Suppose you shot and killed someone and it was an innocent party?"

Mitch's eyes narrowed. The tension was tangible in the room.

"What are you getting at, Captain?"

"Suppose someone had fucked up? Suppose someone had gotten antsy, maybe spinning off from my own hysteria? Then what?"

"You weren't hysterical."

"How can you know when you're hysterical?"

The two men eyed one another warily.

"If you were hysterical, no one would have followed you, Captain. No one would have followed your suggestion to volunteer. We can think for ourselves."

Karoulis lit a rare cigarette, breaking his three-day abstinence, inhaling the smoke deeply into his lungs and letting it seep throughout his body before expelling it in a steady stream. He glanced at Mitch, at once both curious and amazed at the man's composure. "Have you ever killed anyone?" he asked, suddenly.

Mitch stared at him without answering. The smoke coiled in lazy tendrils toward a ceiling fan. The room was eerily silent.

"If I ever kill anyone, Captain, I'll be certain that they deserve it."

"How can you be certain of such a thing?"

"They'd be killers themselves. Or worse. There are worse, you know, Captain."

"You'd be playing God."

Mitch shook his head. "God looks after souls. That's way out of my line. If," he added, "there's a God at all."

Karoulis continued to watch, to study the man before him. He knew he should be chilled, but he wasn't. He was trying to sort out his own reactions to what he was hearing, seeing, and feeling.

Especially to what he was feeling. "How can you be sure that someone's a killer? How can you know? You could make a mistake."

Mitch merely shook his head.

"You can't *know!*"

Mitch looked him straight in the eye. "For the sake of argument, Captain, let's assume that you *can* know. Then what?"

"But you can't know."

"Humor me."

Karoulis licked his lips, took another drag on his cigarette. Then his craggy visage altered suddenly, and he took the cigarette from his lips and stared at Mitch Helwig with dawning understanding. A million images and ideas suddenly welled up in his brain and cavorted about wildly, careening insanely, one against the other. He walked slowly to his desk, found the ashtray under a pile of papers, and methodically ground out the cigarette, still afraid to say what he was thinking. Finally, he turned and gazed long and hard at Mitch Helwig, then managed to mutter, barely audibly, "A Barking Dog."

The words were delivered almost reverently. His thoughts were clearly still far off, still sorting, sifting, weighing.

Mitch said nothing.

Karoulis, too, seemed temporarily stricken speechless. They were riveted in a snapshot-like stillness, suddenly unreal and two-dimensional.

"A Barking Dog," Karoulis repeated.

Mitch had not even blinked.

The silence between them grew and yawned, gradually tightening like a wire being twisted, threatening to snap, to lash back at the two of them dangerously.

"You have one." The senior man's dried lips crackled like kindling in the quiet room.

Mitch said nothing.

Karoulis licked his lips and cleared his throat, deep in thought. He had a sudden, unexpected flashback to his childhood, to a time when he was in short pants and his mother had given him a few coins for candy at a local store. He had been small, very small, and two of the larger boys in the neighborhood had knocked him down, badly scraping his knee, and taken his money. It had been a pathetic kind of childish theft, an act that would cause embarrassment to all concerned for the rest of their lives, no matter how old they grew or how far distant they traveled or lived. The acts of childhood can often be like that—shameful, agonizing, unforgettable. He had had to return to his mother, had had to tell her of his shame, his defeat, to recount with anger and tears his humiliation, and then to make her aware that unless she accompanied him to the store, unless she gave him more coins, he would never get the candy that hung so brightly in his young imagination. The reason that the incident had never been properly put to rest was that his mother had actually questioned his account of the facts, had even suggested that he had fabricated a large portion in order to wrest more money from her mysterious, matronly purse, whence all wealth that he as a boy knew issued.

Even to this day, he felt his cheeks burn at the memory, at the outrage of not being able to prove his tale, to vindicate his plight as a truthful one. And to his own mother.

His mind flickered instantly to his last sight of her in the coffin, eleven years ago, recalling how even then he had wondered if she had ever truly believed him. Or if it mattered.

Then his eyes focused once more clearly and sharply on Mitch Helwig, the man who had dared to step ahead of the pack, the man who didn't seem to care what people thought of him—the man who had made a decision that no one else with his sense of society and integrity, as far as Karoulis knew it and believed it to be, had been able to make.

"Captain." Mitch's voice broke the minute of contemplation.

"What is it, Mitch?"

"You did recommend me for promotion, didn't you?" He gazed blank-faced, a cypher, at the older man.

Karoulis frowned. "You asked me that already, Mitch, not too long ago."

"I'm asking again, Captain."

Karoulis suddenly understood. He could not tell by looking at the bulky uniform in front of him whether or not it hid a Barking Dog. There was no way he could know, unless Mitch actually told him. Then, wildly, he remembered the last time Mitch had asked, recalled vaguely his platitudinous answer, and felt the beginnings of a warm flush creep into his face.

I didn't tell him the truth, he realized. Does he know? Did he have a Barking Dog then? Does he even have one now?

His mother in the coffin. The image welled up, unbidden. It was true, he told her, bending over, I didn't make it up. I want you to believe me. It's important that you believe me, that you know the truth. I want to tell the truth . . .

Mitch was waiting.

The truth.

"Mitch," he began, weakly.

Mitch said nothing.

"I need some time. Can you understand?" He had aged about ten years in the last fifteen minutes.

"Yes, Captain."

"We have to talk again. Perhaps tomorrow, or the next day."

"Yes, sir."

They stood staring at one another. "You can go now, Mitch." His dismissal of Helwig surprised even himself. He just suddenly heard himself saying it, heard it slide forth naturally in response to a deep and powerful need to be alone temporarily with his thoughts, with his feelings.

Mitch stood immobile for a moment, surprised himself. Then he uttered a quick "Thank you, sir," turned, opened the door, and closed it softly behind him.

Outside, he noticed both DeMarco and Huziak viewing him quizzically. He brushed by them, heading for the garage below the station and the closed cocoonlike comfort of his skimmer.

Chapter 24

"Get a load of the ass on that one," Mario Ciracella had observed astutely as they drove down Yonge Street several years ago, trying to separate the hookers from the kids who just wanted to dress like hookers without understanding any of the consequences.

Mitch grunted.

"Wha's that? Some kinda pig noise? Now that's an ass, I tell you. But she's gonna be in big trouble, I tell you."

"How's that?"

"Don't you read the papers?"

"I wait for you to read it to me."

"That I can understand. Well, it seems this babe . . ." He craned his neck to glean one last appreciative look at the bottom that had captured his attention, groaning with deep, soulful wistfulness as it dwindled into his personal history, tracking it to a pinpoint on his side-view mirror.

"You were saying?"

"Ten on a scale of ten," he muttered.

"About the big trouble that fitful young thing is headed for . . ."

"Yeah. Right. Well, it seems that there was this babe who thought she had a brain tumor when her hips and thighs went numb."

"This was in the paper—"

"Right. But it wasn't any brain tumor."

"It was an ass tumor."

"You've got an ass tumor. Only it's spread to your brain.

Comes from sitting right there so much." He nodded, indicating the passenger seat of the cruiser.

Mitch giggled. "I give up. So what was her problem?"

"Tight-fitting jeans."

"Tight-fitting jeans gave her a brain tumor."

"Naw! You're not listenin'. I said she *thought* she had a brain tumor. But it was her tight jeans."

"Well, what'd she have then?"

"There's a tricky medical name for it. Too tricky for you."

Mitch chuckled.

"Problem started because she sat eight hours a day at her job in an orange juice booth. Tight garments trap the nerves, deadening them. The paper said it was a fairly common neurological diagnosis, going as far back as 1885, when girdles first became popular."

"You don't wear a girdle, do you?"

Mario raised one eyebrow, his only concession to having heard the remark. Mitch smiled.

"So," Mitch continued, "do you think it's our duty as law enforcement officers to go back and wrest that young thing from the fiendish clutches of her pants, lest she succumb to the imagined terror of a false brain tumor alarm? Hmmm . . . I see the sense of it. A very humanitarian gesture. Backed by the scientific community . . . By the way, what'd that girl wear while she sat eight hours a day behind that orange juice booth once she'd received her medical diagnosis?"

"I guess she wore no pants. Just think of it, eight hours a day, squeezin' oranges, with no pants on."

"I am thinking of it."

"So am I."

They both smiled.

"Is this what havin' a pregnant wife does to you, Helwig?"

"What?"

"Make you think about girls behind orange juice booths with no pants on."

"Among other things, yes."

"What do you do about it?"

"Squeeze your own oranges."

They both laughed, Mario almost choking on his high-pitched cackle. "Frenchmen dream about women without underwear, you know," he added finally.

"Was this in your paper, too?" Mitch asked incredulously.

"*Psychology Today.*"

"Jesus, Ciracella, you never cease to amaze me with your wide erudition—"

"Angela subscribes," he interjected with a shrug.

"Frenchmen dream of women with no pants . . . A potentially earth-shaking discovery. What do you dream of?"

"Italy is very close to France."

Mitch hooted.

"*Very* close."

"O.K, O.K., so I get it. Pregnancy lasts a long time, doesn't it? How much longer?"

"A month."

"Think you'll make it?"

"If I can find that girl selling orange juice."

They both chuckled, having run the joke for all it was worth, and they proceeded in silence for a while.

"Look at them," Mitch said, breaking the quiet and nodding toward a trio of platinum-bleached hookers in high heels and skin-tight jeans, idling outside the Zanzibar beneath the gaudy yellow and blue marquee. "Beauties, huh? Plenty of brain tumors there."

Instead of responding with a typical one-line, Mario sat pensive, looking straight ahead. Taken aback somewhat, Mitch also remained quiet, letting whatever was on his partner's mind work its way through. His moods were swinging wildly, Mitch had noted lately. But that was to be expected, with Angela eight months pregnant and his life about to alter permanently. In fact, emotional unevenness would constitute the norm, especially in his friend.

But this had the feel of something more.

Mitch waited for Mario to talk. Finally, he did. Without taking his eyes from the road, without taking his hand from the wheel, he told him. "I went with a hooker." His tone remained flat. "Last week."

Mitch said nothing. There was nothing to say. He just listened.

"Got tired of squeezing my own oranges."

The silence fell between them. Mitch wasn't sure that he wanted to hear what he had just heard; but it didn't matter. He had heard it. And from his best friend. He let him continue.

"It's not like Angela wasn't willing, or anything like that. She's great. She'll do anything for me." A wan smile appeared momentarily from beneath the bushy moustache, then disappeared just as swiftly. "It was me that stopped having sex with her. I was afraid of hurting her, of hurting the baby. You understand?" His appeal was weak, but sincere.

Mitch nodded. "I understand."

"But I was going crazy. I felt like a teenager again, jerking off all the time. But you gotta do something, right?"

Mitch nodded again, remembering it all, recalling the wild internal conflicts of guilt, desire, and compassion that eddied up uncontrollably during Elaine's last months. He lowered his head. What was happening to his friend was anything but unique; it was a universal, haunting time that all men shared. And it was as uniquely male as carrying the child for nine months was uniquely female. We all, Mitch knew, handle it in our own way. But we all have to handle it. It's there to be dealt with. Somehow.

"I think maybe being raised a Catholic is the worst of it. Us and the Jews—we got the monopoly on guilt, I think. Don't know what it is. . . . Anyway, last Thursday night, on my last night off, I think I went crazy or something. Told Angela I was going out for a drink, and maybe some fresh air. She knows I'm restless, so it was no big deal. I go out and I have a drink downtown, at the Satin Slipper. I have three drinks. I get to brooding. I'm horny. I'm anxious. I have a fourth drink. There are hookers in the bar, slidin' up and down off them stools, flashin' leg and cleavage, painted up red and yellow and slinkin' around to drive you nuts. One of 'em catches me lookin' and smiles. I smile back. She slips off that stool like she's practiced it all her life, and comes for me. I got to admit"—he paused, sighing—"I was bubbling good by the time she got to me, and I guess she knew it.''

Mario made a left at Shuter, cruising steadily eastward. The story continued to ooze out, as though a button had been pushed. "She sits down. 'Lonely?' she asks. I say 'Yes.' 'Want some company?' she asks. I say, 'How much?'" Mario laughed now, nervously. "Just like in the movies, eh?''

Mitch didn't know what to say. So he said nothing. It seemed best.

"Sixty-five for a blowjob, she says, or eighty-five for a lay. Half-and-half is a hundred. That's what she said. Exactly. Then she waited, smiling. And I waited, too—to hear what I was going to say. I was afraid what I was going to say. And then I heard myself saying it: 'Whereabouts?' 'I got an apartment I share with my girlfriend on Maitland,' she says. 'We could go there. We could talk about it on the way.' So we go,'' Mario said, with an air of finality. "I went up to her dump of an apartment with her, like *I* was in a movie or something. You know?''

The question was rhetorical. Mitch wasn't sure he knew at all.

"She opens the door to her apartment and there's this great fucking Doberman standing inside, in the entranceway. He starts to get up and come toward me, and she shouts for him to go back and sit down. By Christ, I'll tell you I was glad he did. I'll tell you, I looked at her with new respect after that. Havin' him around seemed like sound business practice—a real professional touch. For the first time, though, I felt like a trick. What I was doin' became clearer to me—but only partially. If it had sunk through my thick, hormone-riddled skull thoroughly, I'd have walked out the door right then. But,'' he added, "I didn't. That was where it probably all changed, though.''

Mitch looked at him then.

"We'd decided on a lay on the way over, since she'd told me

that she'd only do blowjobs if the guy was wearing a safe. That made absolutely zero sense to me, since I was the guy who needed the stimulation, and that idea struck me as about as appealing as eating a corned beef sandwich without taking the waxed paper off.''

Dropping his eyes, Mitch shook his head, a rueful smile surfacing. Poor goddamn Mario, he thought. Fished in so completely by a pro—right down to the withdrawn promise of oral delight. She had had no intention, he was certain, of dawdling with this one. Finish him fast, and get back on the streets. Or the bars. Or wherever.

"Said she'd only lay me if I wore a safe, too. Hygiene and stuff. That made a certain amount of sense to me, too, even from my position. And using a safe for gettin' laid isn't all that new to me. I could handle that. I didn't want no AIDS neither." He pushed his hat back on his head, running his fingers through the curly mop of hair that sprang forward.

"So what happened?" Mitch asked, finally.

"Nothing."

Mitch looked at his partner questioningly.

"Nothing to speak of, anyway." He sighed, continuing to tease the hair at the front of his cap. "She took her clothes off, I took my clothes off. I couldn't get it up for a while. She tried to help. Finally, it's up. She slips the safe on it, I slip it into her, and I hump around on top of her for a while. Pretty soon, it falls down again." He paused again. "And I know it isn't going to go back up."

"Why?" Mitch knew why.

Mario shrugged, embarrassed. "It was all just too ridiculous. It was a mistake. You know?"

"I think so."

"The apartment was a dump. A tiny bachelor—mattress on the floor of the living room, bedding everywhere. If you looked at the kitchen area, dirty dishes, even a box of goddamn cornflakes lying

on its side, spilled all over the counter. TV's still on. Jesus. Goddamn Doberman lookin' up my ass, too, don't forget!''

It was almost funny. Mario knew it as well. It was almost
tragic, and he knew that, too.

''It wasn't what I thought, you know?''

''Doesn't sound like my fantasy either.''

''I was stupid, Mitch. Just stupid.''

''We're all stupid, sometimes. You can't lay claim to that all by
yourself.''

''I mean, what the hell was I thinking of? *What* the *hell* was I
thinking of?'' His right hand had come into dramatic motion now,
gesticulating helplessly.

''What'd the hooker say?''

''I'll give her that. She never laughed or nothing. I told her my
wife was pregnant, that I thought I could do it, but I guess I
couldn't. She was pretty good about it. Besides,'' he added, ''I'd
already paid her. And you know, it never did seem like her fault.
It was mine. I mean, I was the one with the problem. Not her.
Right?''

Mitch shrugged. ''Sounds like you solved your problem,
Mario.''

For the first time, Mario looked at his partner, and the look in
his eyes was one of relief, of gratitude that he'd been able to tell
someone, and that that person hadn't belittled him.

''What'd you do then?''

''I drove her back to the Satin Slipper, dropped her off, told her
to take care of herself.''

Neither said anything more for a few blocks. At Parliament
Street, they turned north. Then Mario asked, ''Do you think what I
did was rotten? Do you think I was unfaithful?''

Mitch shook his head. ''You're the only one who can answer
that, Mario. I can't. I'd be inclined to classify it more as a mistake
than anything else, though, if that's of any help to you.''

''Yeah,'' said Mario, mulling it over. ''Yeah.''

Mitch knew that he wasn't particularly good at hearing this type of confession or confidence, and that there was probably much more he should say. The responsibility of the role gradually enveloped him. He tried once more: "It's how you *feel* about these things that counts. In here." He punched a closed fist at his heart. "Not what you *think* about them. Nobody ever stayed up all night worrying over an intellectual problem. At least, nobody normal. Nobody I'd beat down a door to spend time with." He looked out the window. "That's why you couldn't do it, why it wouldn't work."

"You think hearts can feel?"

"Don't know. Something does."

"Yeah. Something." A pause. "There's this lady that's been goin' to the same gynecologist and obstetrician as Angela—she had her baby two nights ago. They didn't think she was going to make it."

"The mother or the baby?"

"The baby. Little girl."

"What happened?"

"The little girl's heart was undeveloped on one side. Born that way. Would have died within days."

"Would have?"

"Yeah. They gave her one of those baboon hearts. Those fuckin' baboons are good for something, besides beating off in the jungle and eatin' fleas offa each other."

"Suppose it'd been your daughter. Would you have let 'em put a baboon heart in her?"

"Fuckin' right I would. Anything that'd save a baby—especially mine—I'd do. I'd gut the fuckin' baboon myself, if I had to. There are no rules for these things, Helwig. You go with what works, with what's right. That's what fuckin' science is for!"

Mitch found himself nodding in complete agreement. You had to break new ground, he knew, to do what was right. If you could see it clearly. If you had the technology.

"I mean," Mario continued, "do you think the kid's got any

less heart, if you know what I mean, simply because it's from a baboon? That she'll grow up somehow lacking feelings that other kids have got? That what's in your heart is somehow tied to the physical hunk of flesh itself?''

"No," said Mitch. "I don't think that at all." He let an interval of silence fall. "Not at all."

Chapter 25

At eight years of age, Barbie Helwig managed to travel the few blocks between Thorncliffe Public School and the apartment block that she called home in the usual time of twenty-five minutes. This entailed stopping and checking each garbage can, as casually as possible, on the off-chance there was a treasure, some rare form of foolishly cast-off exotica therein; one also had to walk only on the pavement cracks for the first block, so as not to tumble to a horrible death in the quicksand, while managing never to step on a crack for the next two blocks, lest one break the sorcerer's magic spell and let loose the multitude of fanged demons that were the inevitable result. It was a tricky—and time-consuming—business. An eight-year-old's itinerary was circuitous at best.

Nevertheless, eyes wide and bright, she arrived in effervescent, wind-blown fashion in the building foyer, decided to buzz for the door to open, in case Mommy was home, thus saving her the trouble of rummaging about in her ever-brimming pockets for her key. It always seemed worth a chance.

"Yes?"

She recognized the voice, with some sense of let-down. It was Mrs. Chan.

"It's me. Barbie." She waited a moment. The buzzer sounded,

and with the usual mighty pull, she opened the door and headed for the elevator. The fact that Mrs. Chan was upstairs meant that Mommy wouldn't be home for a while, she knew. This disappointed her, in a way she did not clearly understand. Mrs. Chan was certainly nice enough. In fact, it didn't seem to have anything to do with Mrs. Chan when you got right down to it. It had to do with Mommy's absence. It had to do with the fact that Barbie felt more and more—what was the word she was searching for?— abandoned? That seemed too strong. Mommy never abandoned her. Neither did Daddy. Yet they were seldom home, especially together, except on occasional weekends.

Barbie had learned to keep herself happy and amused. She made up games, played with her computer, read comics—sometimes even got immersed in a book, although Daddy always told her that a real book was something that didn't start out as a TV show first, something she didn't fully understand at all. For this reason, she had never shown him her favorite: *The Scimitar's Revenge*. It had a picture of Rod McLoughlin, her absolute *favorite*—a real dreamhunk, as Lottie Patel in her class would say—dressed in his scimitar, urban-guerrilla outfit, with a dark-eyed, raven-haired beauty at his side, similarly clad, a beret pulled low on her forehead, as they ventured out into the city to do battle with the proponents of evil. He looked better on the cheap paperback cover than he did on TV; certainly more real, more tangible. A lot of the words she didn't understand. But she readily absorbed the basic fantasy and enjoyed the excitement of it all immensely. It seemed deliciously removed from her self-contained life in the apartment.

She was sure that neither Daddy nor Mommy would approve. But it didn't matter. They'd never know. They weren't around enough to see her struggling through the fascinating world between the shiny covers. It was her secret. Something that was hers, and hers alone.

The elevator door slid open, and she scurried down the hall. She wondered what Mrs. Chan would make for dinner.

Chapter 26

The veal at La Cantina had been superb; the Chianti, exquisite. The conversation had been stimulating, heightened by the dim lighting, the flickering shadow of that ominous candle on the checkered tablecloth, and the sense of anticipation that hovered in the air between them like a tangible thing. When the waiter cleared the table, they were both crisply aware of the next hurdle to be leapt. They managed to stave it off in as pleasant a manner as possible by ordering coffee and liqueurs.

"What's on the agenda tomorrow?" Elaine asked. Even as she asked it, she wondered if some inner control center had caused her to make a psychic vault over what was still on the agenda for this evening. Sticking to shoptalk was, she realized, probably some form of denial of what she was really doing here, what they were both doing here.

What would probably happen . . .

"Two things. Going to take some samples of the new software programs that those two psychiatrists from Buffalo came up with over to a group of doctors at Toronto General. The meeting's set for ten o'clock." He lifted the Cointreau to his lips, sipped, smiled with satisfaction, looked at Elaine lingeringly. He replaced it on the table. She let him talk. "These guys have written programs that can help people think their way out of phobias by using their subconscious—hypnotize themselves, virtually."

"Is there a market for this?" she asked, not without some wryness.

"We think so. Now we're going to find out."

"Your computer can be your shrink."

He nodded. "To some extent, they've convinced us."

"How?" she asked, interested in spite of herself.

"People," he said, "are of two minds about nearly everything." He looked her in the eye. "Haven't you noticed?"

"Yes," she said. "I have." She let the silence say the rest.

"Everyone has an unconscious mind as well as a conscious one. The unconscious one keeps a record of everything we've ever seen, every skill we've ever learned, every judgment we've ever made. All this is inside the brain—if we could just get at it. The key to making these programs work is the user's ability to go into a trance." He looked displeased with the word "trance." He tried again. "Not really a trance . . . more like managing to block out all other thoughts and concentrate your attention on one source of information. 'Trances' can be shallow or deep and still fit the name; it's at this point, though, that it's possible to get information either into or out of the unconscious mind."

"Closer to meditation? To Zen?"

"If you can do that, you could use these programs, I'd warrant. At least that's what the gents down at Toronto General want to satisfy themselves about before ordering a pile. They're hooked on the theory. We're going to see if they can actually use it."

"How does it work? I mean, is it run on a video component? Or with printed messages? Or what?"

"The first demos we've got operate on printed messages. If they succeed, we'll escalate the programs by allotting more funds to their development. Eventually, there'd be a video component, with accompanying audio interaction—quite sophisticated."

"I'll say. Settle back, folks, plug in your Shrink 5000, and explore your navel."

He chuckled. "Next step is marketing and pricing."

"Expensive?"

"Of necessity, yes."

"Why? Expensive to produce them?"

"No. People won't take them seriously unless they cost a lot. Our marketing research has confirmed this. They'll sell much better at, say, a hundred and twenty dollars than they would at sixty.''

''That's crazy.''

''That's human nature.''

''Isn't that a little cynical?''

''Not at all. It's a free market. No one has to buy. No one,'' he added, ''can make us do anything we don't want to do, unless they subject us to some sort of coercion, can they?'' He sipped his Cointreau, smiling mischievously.

She, too, smiled mischievously. ''Not as long as we're all of two minds about everything anyway.'' She sipped her Bailey's, letting it glow within her. Then she reached across and placed her hand on his. ''You said there were two things on the agenda for tomorrow. What's the second?''

''Lunch with you.''

She smiled, as his finger traced her wrist sensuously. In spite of the pleasure, the anticipation, she was still nervous—a tingling of uncomfortable tension, not unlike a form of vertigo. What she was doing was dizzying. There was no precedent in her experience for the ascent to the lofty heights of risk and passion she was contemplating. *People,* she heard him say once more in her head, *are of two minds about nearly everything.* Her subconscious dredged up fleeting images of her wedding day, of an early date she had gone on with Mitch, of sitting in the middle of the night breast-feeding Barbie, listening to rain come down onto the parking lot pavement outside their apartment window, feeling at peace with herself. Where had it all gone?

She didn't know.

They had bridged the subject of this evening wordlessly. But they would be together. That much she knew. It seemed to be inevitable. It was what she wanted, she told herself.

Briefly, she saw the flame from the candle glint in the gold ring on her left hand.

* * *

When they had finished making love, they lay side by side on their backs, their hands clasped. It had been good for both of them. Elaine turned her head and stared at Don's profile, silhouetted against the flashing neon from the sign of the Lakeshore Motel, not far from their window. He was breathing regularly, his eyes closed, a look of contentment on his shadowed features. She turned on her side to face him, resting her free hand on his chest, caressing him lightly. He turned to her, cupping her bare shoulder, sliding his hand along her arm and down to her breast, stroking it gently, lovingly, touching the nipple sensuously and delicately so that it began to harden again. Then he touched his lips to hers and she kissed him back, and they moved once more into one another's arms, giving and receiving the comforts of the flesh, seeking solace.

They stayed like that for a long time, having already spent themselves physically. It was only when she felt the wetness of the pillow, then realized that it was coming from the tears streaming silently down her cheeks, that she rolled away and sat up. He touched her back. She stood up, shivering, and reached down for her bra and pants, ignoring as best she could the fact that the tears, which had sprung so surprisingly from deep and quiet springs, were still flowing, dreamlike, down her face.

Chapter 27

When Mitch arrived home around 12:30 A.M., both weary and tense, he was not ready to sleep. Nor was he ready to talk. For this reason, he satisfied himself with a quick glance into his bedroom, where he saw the familiar shape of his wife in their bed; she stirred in a way that suggested she was still awake, and even possibly waiting for him. But he couldn't handle anything like normal communication just yet. He wanted to be left alone for a bit longer—long enough to feel totally exhausted; long enough not to have to think, to justify his every action, to explain every decision he made. His last hour at the station had been spent filling out reports concerning a break-in, a traffic accident, and his decision to take a shot at a mugger who had beaten an eighty-four-year-old woman unconscious for fifty-three dollars.

Firing your revolver could mean paperwork for hours, he knew. His only regret was that he had missed. It was merely incidental that the woman had not died; she had been meant to die. Or if not, it had certainly been of no particular concern to the mugger either way.

Mitch would have liked to have cornered him alone, out of the way of prying eyes. As he walked down the hall to Barbie's room, he felt the firm presence and shape of the Barking Dog on his belt, beneath his coat.

Opening the door carefully, he peered in. She was asleep, as only children can be, he thought. The covers were tossed aside and she was almost sideways in her bed. He smiled and entered stealthily. He straightened her while she ground her teeth, pulling the covers flush with her chin. Her mouth was opened temporarily, then she ground her teeth again, while he winced at the sound, and turned on her side, her back to him. Polka Bear fell to the floor, and he bent to retrieve it, placing it high on the pillow beside her, then he retreated silently from the room, pulling the door shut behind him. There was, he knew, something infinitely satisfying and peaceful about that room—something that could never be duplicated by the shaping and decorating and guile of an adult's sleeping quarters. A last refuge, he thought, as he walked toward the living room, undoing the brass buttons on the front of his coat. A place where you can still have Polka Bear sleeping with you, and where Daddy can still tuck you in.

Plopping himself in front of the tube, his feet stretched out in front of him on the worn green hassock, he picked up the remote and the TV sprang to life at the touch of his finger. Muting the sound so as not to disturb the others, he let his fingers dance across the pressure buttons at random, while before his eyes jumped glimpses of a multitude of glossy worlds: "A.M. Magazine," "Business Report," the New York Philharmonic, airline schedules, stock quotations, Mr. Grocer Shopping Bargains, a Detroit Red Wing hockey game, a news-weather-sports report in tri-color; along with these were the syndicated ghosts from the past, shows that never died, that instead were sent to wander like the Jew of legend across the electron particles of TV screens the world over, seeking release into death, but never finding it, never meeting their savior, never atoning fully for their original impudent gestures to the world. Mitch was, as always, both horrified and fascinated at stumbling into this world of the walking dead, this realm of post-midnight ghouls—even the eternal "Mary Tyler Moore Show," with Ted Knight recounting for the millionth time how it all began in a five-thousand watt station, flickered briefly on the screen before his finger could press it into temporary oblivion. They skittered across the visual landscape in tumbling succession: "Mad Max," "Santa Barbara," "Video Singles," "Pink Punk," "Maude," "Dallas," "Banana Splits," "Dune . . ."

Ghosts.

Abruptly, his eye caught something in black-and-white flit by, and he willed his hand to halt, then pressed the reverse button until it reappeared.

He sat stunned as he realized what he had stumbled upon. It was an old episode of "Leave It to Beaver." The ludicrousness of airing it at this time hit him first. Then he was smitten with the pleasure of having found it. There they were: the Beaver, Wally, Ward, and June Cleaver—the model North American family of forty or fifty years ago.

How many of them, he wondered, are dead now? How many of them are literally ghosts now?

Everything else about what he was watching was dead, too, he realized. This was the past—the not-very-distant past at that. He

watched the Beaver swing around the white picket fence that sur-
rounded his house—a Cape Cod style, detached—his baseball cap
swiveled at a careless angle on his tousled head, his eyes bright
and dancing, his schoolbooks under his arm. He was talking with
Lumpy. The dialogue was typical: "Gee, Lumpy, I don't
know . . . If I had my choice between a three-pound bass and a
girl, I'd take the three-pound bass."

Ghosts.

Mitch Helwig sat and watched the whole episode, scarcely moving. When it ended, he pressed the off button and sat for a long
time in the dimly lit room. It was two o'clock before he decided to
go to bed.

Chapter 28

That night, Barbie dreamed, among other things, of living in a big
house in some unidentifiable part of the city, a house riddled with
secret passages and underground tunnels and innumerable rooms.
In one of the rooms was Ms. Lowry, her third-grade teacher. In
another were Gramp and Gram Helwig, and the room smelled just
like their house always did: pipe tobacco and gumwood. Another
room was tilted like the Magic Carpet Ride at the Exhibition, another rolled and swayed like the SeaRoom at ElectroWorld. In her
dream, she and Lottie Patel, her best friend, spent their time hunting for the key to the attic, because they knew that up there was
where the Scimitar was being held captive, and they had to free
him.

* * *

Mitch Helwig, for the most part, slept dreamlessly, except for a brief flurry of REM activity around dawn. When he awoke, all he could recall was a tangle of images woven together in a patternless jumble, like a ball of yarn hopelessly knotted. He remembered, though, watching the Beaver in his dream, down at the station with Karoulis, DeMarco, Elaine, and Mario. The Beaver was going to shoot Lumpy out of a cannon.

Elaine Helwig did not dream at all that night.
For that matter, she did not even sleep.

Chapter 29

"He's there again, Mr. Scopellini." Daniel Otis spoke into the intercom handset, standing in the privacy of the large, tinted second-story window that faced out onto Commercial Road. He was gazing down at the dark brown, late-model Chevrolet discreetly parked a block or so down the street, scarcely noticeable in the waning twilight.

"You're sure it's the same car?"

"Yes, sir. Even parked in the same place."

The Archangel frowned. A complication. He didn't like complications.

"Thank you, Daniel." He paused in thought. It was the fifth time the tail had been spotted. What was going on? What did he want? A lone cop, off-duty . . . And all he did was follow him home, then disappear into the night. They hadn't been able to make sense of it yet.

"Same thing tonight, then, Daniel. You and Charles follow in separate vehicles. Just surveillance. Don't alert him to your presence. If he tries to stop me, or come anywhere within any kind of threatening distance, intercept and apprehend. Don't harm him, if possible, but use your good judgment. Be prepared to eliminate him if necessary. But you know what I want . . . I want to know what he's up to. Does he represent the police, or some other group, or is he acting alone? Follow him home, if he leaves me as he has done before. Stake out his apartment. Bring me all and any information that you have on him by noon tomorrow. All right?''

"Yes, Mr. Scopellini."

"Good. You know what to do, then.''

"Yes, sir.''

The Archangel lifted his finger from the console button he'd been holding down, still frowning. They had gotten the man's name after they had spotted him the first time: Mitch Helwig. He was, so he understood from Otis and Purdon, the subject of a growing file folder, which the Archangel hoped would be complete by tomorrow noon.

But he didn't like it. None of it. It stank of a kind of fanaticism that mere money might not be able to salve over. He thought of the number of cops, judges, court and city hall officials that were on his payroll, about the tentacles he had into all aspects of the city and its enforcement and judiciary systems, about how he had nothing to fear from anywhere. People had only things to gain by allowing him large and gracious elbowroom; there was nothing to gain by harassing him—unless the harasser was impervious to the common sense of personal gain.

And it was this last thought that worried him. He knew that such people—such righteous, inflexible, shrill, and idealistic bantams— did indeed exist, but his path had not crossed with theirs. Not to date, anyway.

But he had known there was always the chance—indeed, the probability—that it had to happen eventually. But this lone wolf, this, this . . . Helwig . . . was not what he had pictured. Not at all.

A muscle in his neck knotted. His hand rose slowly and pa-

tiently and massaged it, knowing that all such knots could be exor-
cised by careful, patient manipulation.

He considered Mitch Helwig such a knot.

His fingers pressed firmly into his flesh. He rotated his head
carefully, waiting for the cramp to subside.

It was still there when he went down to his car at six o'clock.

Chapter 30

Mitch spotted his tail shortly after following Arcangelo Scopellini
onto the Don Valley Parkway: the sleek, dark blue Buick, three
cars back. He was sure of it. What he wasn't sure of was whether
it was the only one, or what it planned to do about him.

A half-grin of wry satisfaction appeared momentarily, then vanished. It was what he had been waiting for. Finally, he thought.
They were beginning to show themselves. For the last three evenings, he had performed the ritualistic tracking of the Archangel to
his lair, waiting to flush out someone who might be of use to him.
He had considered it virtually without question that he would be
spotted soon. The surprise was that it had taken them so long. Or,
he mused, perhaps they were better than he thought they were, and
they'd had him under surveillance since the beginning, and he had
just noticed them. And although the idea gave him no comfort, he
did not discredit it completely. He was dealing, after all, with con-
summate professionals, not back-alley punks.

In style, anyway, he told himself.

Elaine had wanted to talk to him tonight, he knew, when she
got home from work—which would be any time now. And he
wouldn't be there. Again. He didn't know what to do about that
part of his life. I've got to deal with it, he thought. It's slipping

away, disintegrating. His mind pictured a sand castle after a wave had receded, melting into formlessness, ebbing out with the motion of the water.

It was his marriage. Then, in an instant of coldness, the follow-up occurred to him: *it's my life.*

The wide Cadillac ahead of him changed lanes, forcing his mind back to the present, clearing his head to the hard shapes and pressures of the slippery world about him. He glanced out his side window at the car on his left, noting the driver briefly, struck with his ordinariness. The automobile world surrounding him at this instant, gliding in purple darkness and white quartz headlight beams at one hundred kilometers an hour, was an analog of the world in general, he thought. Most of us are only concerned with going home after putting in our time for someone else, loosening our collars, pouring the preprandial drink, watching the news, closing the door on the outside world, chatting with our mates, with our kids, eating a meal with people who aren't merely utilizing us for the greater good of the Company.

Ordinary.

And in the midst of this mundaneness, there are predators like the Archangel and his cohorts behind me, he thought. Camouflaged; invisible. Gliding smoothly with the urban flow at twilight, unnoticeable to the untrained eye, blending into the picture unassumingly. They even blink properly when they change lanes, he thought. Trying to appear ordinary, like the others, on the surface.

And there is me, he knew. But I'm the only one like me. I, too, can blend. Because I'm alone.

He changed lanes, too. Glancing in his rear-view mirror, he saw the dark blue Buick slide laterally as well—signaling courteously and safely, of course.

Beside him, on the seat, were the two laser pistols—the Bausch & Lomb and the domestic one he had taken from the punk in the alley that night.

Blending. Flowing . . .

The Cadillac veered off at York Mills, heading east. Just a man going home, thought Mitch. After a hard day at the office fencing stolen lasers, stolen cars, distributing dope, making stolen hand-guns and sundry assault weapons available to the needy, eliminating anyone who was inconvenient enough to slow down business in general . . .

What else, he wondered, went on in that warehouse? During his limited stakeout, he hadn't been able to determine all of the multi-faceted nature of the business. What he had determined was the scope of the traffic and trade: it was vast. He had seen tractor-trailers and semis from most provinces and dozens of states unload and load. The distribution and movement of goods—whatever they were—were not merely local, but international and large-scale. This man, the Archangel, was no trifler, Mitch knew. He was worth hunting, worth bringing down. He was big. *Big.*

All of which had made Mitch wonder on occasion how and why he had been permitted to operate so brazenly and profitably for so long, without any sort of pressure from authorities. Surely it was known that he was here, that he was operating.

Mitch thought he knew the answer, though; and he didn't like the answer. *Fear and money.* That was the answer. How many people were afraid of him? How many people had he bought?

How many people had a vested interest in seeing the Archangel protected, at almost any cost?

And how many would do almost anything to eliminate Mitch Helwig, if they had even the most remote idea what was playing about in his head?

Mitch felt himself alone again in the flowing traffic.

The Cadillac turned onto the Archangel's street. Mitch let it precede him at a safe distance, then followed around the corner. A block later, he glanced in the rear-view mirror to assure himself that the Buick was coming. It was. A block farther, he caught what he thought was a second set of headlights turn the corner, from the same direction. Coincidence? he wondered. Perhaps. But don't think of it that way, he told himself. Think the worst. Be prepared.

The Archangel glided into his driveway. A minute later, as he was getting out of his car, Mitch Helwig drove by silently. The Archangel stood, carefully, behind the door he was still holding open, watching, as first Daniel Otis and then Charles Purdon a minute later, slid by and faded into the night, their quarry in sight. Watching the three sets of red taillights disappear, the Archangel smiled briefly, then turned and went into the house.

Tonight, he thought, I feel like having a woman. He thought of Eveline, his favorite, of her smooth white thighs, her long legs, her perfect breasts, her exquisite mouth. Inside, he poured himself a rye and water, removed his gray jacket, unbuttoned his vest, and sighed down onto the leather sofa. He took a sip, placed it carefully on the coaster on the smoke-glass end table, and picked up the phone.

She'll be here, he thought, by nine.

Mitch made a right at the next stop sign, then another right, and eventually made a left onto York Mills Road, heading west, back to the Don Valley Parkway. The two sets of headlights that were stalking him disappeared smartly from his rear-view—further evidence, thought Mitch, that these were pros. They didn't make the obvious mistakes of amateurs by insisting on keeping him in sight at all times, at the risk of exposure. They knew how to play the odds; to them, it was evident that he was following a familiar pattern—the one he had already established: he would likely head home, as he had done previously. Also, he reflected, there was a chance that the surveillance was even more extensive than he imagined. Right now, for instance, he could be being monitored by someone standing in the darkness on one of the lawns about him, who was in turn keeping the two mobile tails informed of his movements. He knew that he could discount nothing.

Only briefly did the notion that the tails belonged to anyone other than the Archangel occur to him. He remembered his conversation with Karoulis a week ago. Karoulis had not yet summoned him to resume their dialogue. True, he had been off for three days.

Nevertheless, the next-day conversation Karoulis had alluded to had not happened. Had Karoulis put a tail on him? Mitch played with the idea fleetingly, as always, unwilling to discount anything. It was possible. But this didn't feel like Karoulis. Nor did the cars resemble the tails he was familiar with. The Buick was much too new, much too elegant and luxurious to be a part of any traditional police work.

And he had his hunches, his instincts. They all told him he was under the Archangel's watchful eye.

About a mile south of York Mills on the parkway, he picked up the Buick again. Straining, he thought he spotted the second car farther back, judging from the rhythms of speed and lane-shifting that accompanied his own travel. Still, he couldn't make out the type of vehicle; he needed to be much closer for that.

The adrenaline began to pump more freely through his body. He punched on the radio, letting some pulsing, white-hot megachords snap at the stale air in his car, not merely tolerating the sounds that he found so alien, but quietly losing himself in them. Through his front windshield, he became hypnotized by the steady river of red eyes that flowed ahead of him into the dark, serpentine distance. And the left side of his face lit eerily with the shifting shadows of the white beams that streamed like an electric current along the dry riverbed of highway conducting people homeward in the opposite direction.

All those ordinary people, he thought. *And then there's us.*

What surprised Otis, in the dark-blue Buick ahead of Purdon, was when Helwig continued on the parkway past both the Eglinton exit and the O'Connor Street exit, either of which would have taken him home to his Thorncliffe apartment.

Where's he headed? he wondered. The evening had suddenly twisted into quiet life for him, stirring itself from the somnolence that had gripped it so predictably.

He felt his own adrenaline begin to sluice through his strong frame, sensed his night vision sharpen, and smiled a tiny saurian smile. Pressing the button on his intercom, he said, simply, "He's headed downtown."

The metal voice responded: "You're both in sight."

Otis released the button and settled back for the cruise ahead.

Mitch steadily and inexorably led them down the city's central artery, down into its neon and smoke-filled heart.

Chapter 31

It was 6 A.M., according to the bedside digital, when the V-phone had beeped that morning.

"Jesus Christ." He rolled over and clawed at the bedding, surfacing from a deep level-seven dream. The air outside the covers was cold. Goddamn superintendent, thought Mitch. Saving money for some faceless corporate group of fucking moral eunuchs. You can bet nobody turns down the fucking heat in *their* apartments without a memo typed out in illuminated script and suitably notarized. Jesus.

"What's that?" slurred Elaine.

"Phone."

"What time is it?"

"Six."

"Jesus."

"My sentiments exactly. And it better be somebody as important as *Him* on the phone." Swinging his feet over the side of the bed, he sighed loudly, ran a hand through his disheveled hair, and reached across the bedside table to where the phone had gotten shoved sometime in the last week, and then forgotten. He thought he could see his breath in the room, but wasn't sure. It was still too dark.

"Hello." He left the video screen blanked out.

"What do you call people who use the rhythm method for birth control?"

In spite of himself, Mitch found himself beginning to smile. He snorted a half-laugh into the cool, plastic transmitter in his hand.

When that was deemed the only response by the listener on the other end, the answer popped out in Mario Ciracella's inimitable manner: "Parents."

Mitch hooted.

Mario laughed delightedly on the other end.

Elaine propped herself up on one elbow, a perplexed look on her face. "Who is it?"

"It *is* Him. Jesus Christ!"

She smiled tolerantly.

"Where's Jesus Christ?" Mario felt one had been slipped by him.

"Where he's always been. On the dashboards of all your relatives' cars, asshole."

Elaine plopped herself back onto her pillow, smiling more broadly now, even in the darkness. Mitch bantered with only one person that way. She awaited the announcement.

"Do you, uh, by any chance, have any news for us, garlic breath?"

"God, you're witty, Helwig. So fast. So inventive."

"Did you hear about the Italian on trial for armed robbery? The foreman came out and announced the verdict: 'Not guilty.' The little curly-headed paisano leaps to his feet and shouts, 'Wonderful!' kisses his fingers, then turns to his attorney and asks, 'Does this mean I can keep the money?'"

Elaine continued to smile as she listened. Mario could be heard chuckling in the distance, his chortle muted tinnily.

"Boy or girl?" Mitch asked finally.

"The world," announced Mario, "has been blessed by the arrival of Anthony Joseph Paul Ciracella, about an hour ago, weighing in at eight pounds, six ounces. They gave it to me in metric, but I forgot.''

"A boy!"

Elaine sat up and asked, ''How's Angela?''

"Everybody okay?" Mitch translated.

"Everybody's beautiful! He's more handsome than I am, if you can imagine such a thing.''

Mitch nodded and smiled at Angela; then he said into the phone, ''The mind boggles.''

"And I got more news for you, jackass!''

"You're donating your testicles to the Smithsonian Institution, to provide a suitable match for John Dillinger's weapon.''

"Not a bad idea. The world should know what strides among them like a colossus.''

"So what's the news?''

"You're gonna be the godfather. Elaine's gonna be the god-mother.''

Mitch suddenly had no retort for this. The seriousness of the concept filtered through to him, along with the honor. ''I'm over-whelmed,'' he said, truthfully.

"I know you're overwhelmed. You damn well should be. And you do agree, right?''

A couple of thoughts occurred to him, like flashes in the night, and they spilled out of him. ''I'm not a Catholic, Mario. Isn't that important to you?''

"No.''

"But won't it be important to the priest, or to the family at large, or to somebody?''

"We won't tell them.''

"Suppose they ask!''

"We'll lie.''

Mitch was perplexed. ''Is this really what you want?''

"Fuckin' right, it is.''

"And Angela, too?''

"Her, too."

Mitch felt a hand on his shoulder. He turned to Elaine. "We're going to be godparents to Anthony Joseph Paul." He smiled.

Her eyes widened with delight. "Wonderful!"

"Elaine approves," he said into the phone.

"Good girl. Good sense. No stupid questions like you."

"Mario?"

"Mmm?"

"Are there any saints' names you left out?"

"Yeah. Polycarp, asshole. Oh yeah, and Mitch. Saint fuckin' Mitch. Good Vatican name, that. Jesus. I ride with a religious lightweight. No culture. No tradition."

Mitch laughed. "You're not smart enough to have a son. I told you all about it, remember?"

"I'm donatin' my balls to the Smithsonian, after I've finished with 'em, remember? Check in on 'em."

"When'll that be?"

"In about a hundred fuckin' years." It was his turn to hoot. Mitch had to hold the phone away from his ear.

"Listen, Mario—congratulations, really. It's great."

Mario accepted the congratulations with modest silence this time.

"And we'll be down to see Angela and Anthony this evening. Is that okay?"

"We'll all be there. But listen, Mitch, when you address my son in future, I think it best you stick to his *real* name."

"What's that?"

"What else? Tony!"

"Of course! What else?"

Mario was silent again. Then: "Mitch?"

"Yeah?"

"Was it this exciting for you? With Barbie? Is it always like this?" There was that genuine note of candor in his voice that sprang to the surface spontaneously every so often. Mitch had often both envied and admired it. It was what ingratiated Mario to

him and to others. He would open himself to you, trust himself
with you, with an honesty and vulnerability that Mitch knew he
himself did not possess. Mario, he had often thought, is simply a
nicer guy than I am. And I'm glad to be his friend.

"Mario," he said, finally. "It's the pinnacle. If we live to be a
hundred and fifty, there may never be anything as good. Understand?"

"Yeah. Yeah, I do. Thanks, Mitch."

"Get some sleep. And congratulations again. Say hello to Angela for us. See you tonight."

"Mitch?"

"What is it now?"

"I think I found what I'm not looking for." This time, Mitch
noted, he did not giggle as he recited Angela's thesis title. It was
the first time.

"And Mitch?"

"Yes, Mario?" he answered patiently.

"I'm gonna call Max."

"Max?"

"Max Rosen. In Greenland."

"You're gonna call *Green*land?"

"Why not? You said this is the pinnacle. This is as good as it
gets."

Mitch softened. "You're right. Do it. Call fucking Greenland."
He paused. "And Mario . . ."

"Yeah?"

"Enjoy it. Every minute of it. You deserve it."

"Thanks, Mitch. See you."

"See you." He hung up the phone and sat in the dark for a
minute without moving, until goose bumps finally rose on his
shoulders in the cold room.

"What is it?" Elaine asked.

"Greenland. Fucking Greenland."

Chapter 32

Hovering like iridescent silicon bones, the overhead fluorescents blipped past Mitch's windshield as he eased the Chevrolet up the ramp from the parkway and accelerated west on the Gardiner Expressway. On his left were the faceless, gray shapes of the waterfront warehouses—grain and storage depots holding cargo from the ships that ventured down the St. Lawrence Seaway into the heart of the continent's east. Beyond them, the dark expanse of the inner harbor was lit only by random lights, and farther out, the shoreline lights of the Toronto Islands. He watched as the blinking reds and whites of a small private plane headed down on an angle toward the local Island Airport.

On his right, the landmark sign appeared on the billboard where it had been anchored for thirty years: JESUS SAVES: CALL JIM . . . and a phone number. The bottom left section of paper was hanging disconsolately from the sign, a stilled pendulum on the commercial road to salvation. Perhaps Jim didn't answer anymore, thought Mitch.

He drove on, sliding down the next ramp to the Lakeshore, then onto Queen's Quay, ever closer to the waterfront.

There were two cars, never far behind him.

It's happening, Mitch thought. They're sticking with me.

The adrenaline continued to pump, sharpening and tightening his senses.

Once on Queen's Quay, he pulled into a municipal parking lot, paid the flat evening fee, and maneuvered the Chevrolet into a spot in the midst of hundreds of other vehicles, constantly alert to his shadows. They were not far behind now. First came the Buick, then within seconds came a Lincoln Continental of similar vintage and color; both had been selected, he assumed, for their power, opulence, and lack of outstanding features. They blended nicely, as they were supposed to do.

Mitch checked his digital: 6:55 P.M. The weather for October was about right—nippy and bleak. And it was dark already, as the remnants of daylight saving time sputtered to a grinding halt. The wind off the lake made it even cooler. He pulled the nylon zipper on his Korean-made Impulse jacket to his neck, snapped the buttons tight around his wrists, cut the jarring chords from the radio in half at the same time he cut the engine, then picked up the two lasers from the seat beside him and slipped one into each of his jacket's side pockets, securing them with the Velcro press fasteners.

His two shadows were sliding into berths a couple of aisles away. He watched as their headlights were extinguished, each in turn. The island ferry's foghorn sounded across the harbor.

He breathed deeply and opened the door, stepping out into the night. His heart rate quickened a touch—just enough to pump him full of wary vigilance, to sharpen his alertness. Squinting, he scanned the bleak waterfront, confirming decisions, rerouting others instantaneously. The wind tugged at his jacket and swept a lock of hair the wrong way across his forehead. He ignored it, concentrating instead on his situation, his surroundings, and his plans; ranking priorities clearly, he understood, came from certainty of purpose. And he was certain of his purpose.

Sinking his hands into his pants' pockets against the cold and hunching his shoulders against the wind, Mitch strode out of the parking lot and along the quay toward the ferry entrance. As he passed the lights of the Harbor Castle Hilton he stopped, ostensibly to peruse a sign posted at its entrance. It gave him a chance, though, to glance fleetingly out of the corner of his eye, without fully turning his head, at the pedestrians behind him. He saw them slow their pace, about thirty meters back: two men, with greatcoats done up tightly at the necks. He read the notice of entertainers and lounges with marked indifference, taking just long enough for at least surface credibility, then turned and walked onward into the wind.

At his back, he could feel, without looking, the unhurried pursuit of his dual harriers, and his mouth tightened in a grim line as he clenched his teeth. Come on, you fuckers. Come on. Keep coming. His hands balled into fists inside his pockets.

He turned abruptly left at the west side of the Hilton and headed for the ferries' ticket booths. Only a handful of people were awaiting the boats' arrival at this time of night and in this weather: maintenance personnel, a couple of lovers stuck for a place to be alone, and the few others were probably all headed for the Island Airport. Usually, he thought, the owners of the planes and their associates did not need to rely on public transportation across; perhaps, though, at this time of night . . .

Not that it mattered. Idle speculation. A few residents of the old, dilapidated, city-owned cottages on Ward's Island might be among them. And in a city of two and a half million, there was always somebody doing something that defied rational explanation. I know a lot about that, he thought.

The *Sam McBride* was plunging back across the choppy waters about halfway out, its lights pinpoints in the gray evening. Mitch had chosen it instead of the newer *Ned Hanlan,* which boarded a bit farther west at the new docks. He liked the tradition of the old ferry; he remembered the excitement of day-trips to the Islands with his parents when he was a kid. The *Sam McBride* had always been a part of it. The *Ned Hanlan,* the new hydrofoil, was much more popular, always more crowded, and certainly quicker; for all these reasons Mitch didn't want to use it. He looked around at the other people and wondered again what their reasons were. We wait, he thought, on the edge of the twenty-first century, for a vehicle from the nineteenth century, to carry us to an island that serves no logical purpose anymore. Unless the purpose is personal. He felt the contours of the lasers in his pockets, the security of his Silent Guard under his shirt; then he thought again—bizarrely, he felt—about the times that his parents had taken him across for the day, for relief from the sweltering city, amid the black willows that hemmed the lagoons. He remembered the time his father had rented the quadricycle on Hanlan's Point, and they had all ridden in it to Centre Island and back. He was musing about his inability to give up the past when the *Sam McBride* lowed loudly, drawing him from his reverie.

The two gray shadows behind him bought their tickets and attempted to adopt the casual idleness of those about them. Separating, they loitered at opposite ends of the waiting area, their collars turned up against the chill, masking them partially. One of them lit a cigarette.

Mitch could hear the *Sam McBride* slicing through the waves now, could see its foaming wake, a white V churning madly on black water. A minute later, its engines had stopped, then reversed, as it shuddered its way into berth, its two-storied rings of lights bobbing rhythmically to a halt. The landing planks were positioned; the gates opened. A few passengers disembarked, then the handful surrounding Mitch began to flow through the neck of the gates and onto the lower deck, where they scattered randomly, like billiard balls broken from a clump by a slow-moving white ball. Mitch strode halfway to the front, then sat down, his back to the central wall housing the engines, his eyes staring at his reflection in the windows that kept the cold from total invasion. In his peripheral vision, he saw one man sit down very close to where they had entered; the other appeared a moment later at the vessel's front, apparently having skirted the center section and come around from the other side. He too sat down.

Mitch was between them. He smiled to himself, relaxed, and prepared to enjoy the ride.

Moments after the boat pulled into the Centre Island dock, Mitch rose and walked in the direction of the exit. The shadow ahead of him also rose inconspicuously, and eased into the small group huddled in waiting. Behind him, Mitch knew that the other shadow was also in steady movement. He pressed forward, trying to catch a glimpse of the one ahead of him. A partial success: he noted hawklike features, large, bony ridges shaping the face, as a dull putty knife might carve an apple's interior; a big man, with dirty blond hair, thinning on top. He turned his back flush to Mitch, preventing further inventory.

The gates opened, beckoning them onto the dark terrain of this flat, fragmented bow of shattered prehistoric peninsula, the land masses that had sheltered the former town of York, making of its shoreline a natural haven for shipping, a place where nature embraced the land in open, arms-wide sanctuary.

A place, Mitch was sure, where people would die tonight. Soon. They filed out.

It was cold. But that only served to heighten Mitch's senses. They had been walking about five minutes, Mitch leading his trackers ever farther into the dark isolation of the island's interior. He relished the reversal of roles. Apparently stalked, but very much the stalker, he was acutely aware that the jackals behind him regarded him as merely another unwary prey.

The wire from his Barking Dog tickled his side with the chill of anticipation.

When he reached the far side of the island, he turned right and headed west, in the direction of Hanlan's Point, along the vacant asphalt pathway. There was only a sliver of moon, but it hung brightly over the water, the clouds having been scattered widely by the biting wind. Soon, he knew. Soon.

Some trees up ahead. Yes. And a bend in the pathway.

Without even bothering to check, he knew that they were back there—perhaps a hundred meters, perhaps less—shrouded in the darkness and muffled by the wind and the waves flooding rhythmically up onto the beach nearby. *They feel safe. And hidden.*

Long strands from the black willows undulated weirdly, their tips trailing blindly across the sprouts of dying October grass, swishing noises in the night. Mitch ducked quickly in among them, pressing against the bole of a tree. From there he turned and watched. And waited.

He saw them. Thirty meters. Twenty. He squinted, tensed. There was the one he had identified on the ferry, his thinning blond hair whipping with the wind, his brow beetled. With him came the other man, whom Mitch could see face-on for the first time. Even in the darkness and at a distance he felt their coldness and their menace.

Coldness and menace. The words played in his head. Come and meet your fucking match. Right here. Yes. Here.

The biggest problem was simply that there were two of them. That would be his eventual edge, he knew. But the immediate edge was theirs. He had been hoping they would trail one another with a lengthy interval between, allowing him to deal with them separately. This would be another matter.

Ten meters. Five. No more time.

He reached into his pocket and took out the Bausch & Lomb, feeling a perverse kinship with it. Bonds, after all, are forged with memories and events, and it had served him faithfully.

They passed. As they did so, he stepped silently out from his seclusion within the willow branches onto the pathway, positioned himself firmly, and raised the laser, steadying his right wrist with his left hand.

"Freeze!"

For a moment, they did, stunned at the voice from behind them. Then, it seemed to Mitch, all hell broke loose. In an instant, they rolled in opposite directions, a practiced move that took Mitch by surprise.

He squeezed the trigger. A bolt of blue frost pierced the night, searing the asphalt and the grass as he held the trigger down, arcing his arm in the direction of the one who had rolled off to his right.

A scream! Mitch's heart pounded. He had made contact. He broke into a run, heading for the sound. Within five long strides, he was there, peering over the squirming body of the man whose face he had just seen for the first time only a minute ago. He was clutching his thigh, where the blood was gushing freely over his hands, and his leg was jerking convulsively. His face was contorted in pain, but beneath the pain, the danger was registering, and he let his leg jerk with its severed muscles as he tried desperately to reach inside his greatcoat and withdraw a weapon.

Mitch kicked him full in the face, snapping his head backward. The man sprawled out unconscious on the grass. Blood appeared slowly from his mouth and nose. Bending, Mitch checked his breathing. He was alive, and would stay alive for a while—if he didn't bleed to death. Mitch looked down at the leg. Ripping the coat open on the prone figure, Mitch pulled the flannel scarf from around the neck, and used it quickly and crudely as a pressure bandage, stopping the flow from the thigh as best as he could.

No more than ten or fifteen seconds had elapsed when Mitch stood up and peered into the night in search of the other man, who now matched him in the dark one on one.

He had to move, he realized. *Have to get away from this spot. He knows where I am, but I don't know where he is.*

Out there. Somewhere.

As he moved, a streak of cobalt heat burned into the grass where he had been standing. Mitch broke into a run, leaving as much space between himself and the tracking point of the laser as was humanly possible—as quickly as possible. He knew a blind swing of the beam could cut down prey, just as he had done only moments ago. Lunging forward, he rolled on the grass, making himself as elusive a target as he could. Then he was up, poised on his knees, the Bausch & Lomb in his hand once more, his eyes hunting in the darkness for the source of the beam that had now blinked out.

A sudden gust scuttled leaves along the asphalt—insidious, random scraping. Mitch held his breath, listening hard.

Nothing.

Out there. Somewhere.

Even if Mitch could see him, he didn't want to kill him. Not like this. This was not the plan.

Now anger was surfacing within him, drowning the fear and wariness. Goddamnit! I blew it. Then: No . . . Calmer: Not yet . . . His hand tightened on the laser, his eyes penetrated the gloom. He sidled to his left, keeping in a crouch, moving stealthily to where he might dare a quick dart across the pathway.

Then Mitch saw him. *He* had decided to dart across the pathway to check on his partner beneath the willow tree. Mitch watched without moving, now that he had a fix on his opponent, accepting the whims and reversals of fate without analysis. Sometimes, he knew, there was only what happened; there was no why.

He remained still. Then, when he was certain that he was not being observed, he slipped off into the coal blackness and circled, silently on the grass, to approach from the other side. The man with the face like a carved apple had stood up, suddenly aware that his moment of concern for his partner may have been a tactical error, and froze as he listened.

Mitch froze in response.

The leaves scraped the pathway, eddied and died.

His options: rush the man and tackle him; cut him down right now, while the opportunity existed; shout for him to "freeze," as he had done before, and hope that this time he might be insecure enough to obey; or maybe aim low on his legs, in hopes of bringing him down without killing him, as he had inadvertently done to the man's partner.

Mitch's mind raced through them all, doubling back, leapfrogging forward, trying to foresee consequences, both likely and unlikely, all within the space of a second. Then the man began to move, and instinct took over.

"Freeze!" His own shout took him by surprise. The laser in his hand was targeted on the man standing beside his unconscious accomplice. But he did freeze this time, as did the entire tableau. Even the leaves stopped their rasping slide, and for an instant, in the silence, Mitch felt his body charge with artificial warmth, as a fresh flush of adrenaline was pumped to all his extremities.

The man did not move.

Mitch stepped forward.

Now the stranger saw him, and even in the darkness Mitch could see his eyes narrow with caution. And with hate.

"Hands in the air!"

The man complied.

"Drop the laser." It fell noiselessly from his fingers to the grass.

They stared at one another, separated by no more than five meters.

Then the man smiled, a condescending smile, full of pity and contempt and false bravado. "You're making a big mistake, fella."

Mitch did not reply.

"You hurt my friend. Do you have any idea what kind of payment will be exacted for that?"

"By whom? You?" Mitch bristled. He stepped closer.

Their eyes met. Neither looked away.

"You're in over your head. Way over your head. Maybe we can still forget about all this, if you'll just use some sense and put that thing away."

"I'll put it up your nose and press the trigger, if you do anything but what I tell you to. Understand?"

The man stared hard at him for a minute, then nodded.

Mitch nodded in return, lengthening the silence. The man lying beneath the tree with his leg wrapped in his scarf moaned incoherently through swollen lips. Then he rolled onto his side and moaned again, only this time the sound was more like a keening for the dead, muted and soulful. The wind, which had picked up a bit, seemed to catch the low anguish and caress it eerily.

"Over by your friend," Mitch instructed.

The man moved closer to the prone figure, which was now writhing into a fetal position, becoming slowly aware of its pain

and helplessness. Then, turning, they faced one another again, ignoring the one on the ground.

"What do you want?" the man asked, his hands still spread
open at the level of his chin.

The truth, Mitch thought. That's what I want. "Information,"
he said.

The man shrugged, said nothing.

Like a thunderclap on a sunny day, the needle of light appeared
without warning from the hand of the man twisted into a fetal
position on the ground, striking Mitch full in the chest. And for the
second time in his life, his Silent Guard gave him another
chance—the grace period he had paid for.

One second burned away. Anticipating Mitch's collapse, the
man standing leaned forward, preparing to walk away. When
Mitch did not slump to the ground in death throes, the man's lips
parted as if to voice his disbelief. During the second second, Mitch
could feel the fatal heat, smell the acrid odor as the laser attempted
to eat its way through the unexpected barrier. Like a cobra striking, he swung his own laser toward the man on the ground,
squeezing the trigger vengefully. The sapphire bolt that sprang
from its mouth sought the source of the beam still blistering his
chest for the third consecutive second, tracked it in flaring silence,
and incinerated the hand that was clutching it. The man shrieked in
stunned, searing pain, and the fingers spasmed open, dropping the
laser; the shaft of light disappeared. Mitch swung the laser back to
cover the man standing beside his writhing partner, all in the blink
of an eye.

Breathing hard now, his heart pounding with the exhilaration of
still being alive, Mitch could feel the perspiration on his back and
forehead. The momentary thought flickered through his head:
Nothing is as invigorating as being shot at and missed . . . It was
incredible. His lungs opened fully, and he found himself gasping
long, deep draughts of welcome night air, crisp and cold. His hand
was rock calm, amazingly steady.

The jaw muscles of the man opposite him clenched and unclenched. Mitch saw his eyes telegraph his fear, his understanding. His *respect*. Mitch liked what he saw. The two-man edge had now undeniably shifted to him. The awareness of it hung in the air between them, palpable and sure.

Mitch's nostrils flared, still stung by the fumes from his scorched jacket and shirt. The burn-hole had widened to become a three-centimeter-diameter puncture of charcoal and curling, acrid smoke.

The man on the ground was still twisting and groaning. Mitch looked at him, feeling nothing. Then he looked back at the man he was covering.

"Move away from him."

The man moved.

"That's far enough. Don't move."

The stranger had no intention of moving. Mitch walked over to the man on the grass without taking his eyes from the one with his hands raised.

He glanced down at the injured man, then quickly back at the one at bay.

"Lie down on your stomach."

The man didn't move.

"Or I'll kill you."

The man lay down on his stomach in the cool autumn grass.

"Put your hands behind your back."

Slowly, the hands appeared, clasping one another at the small of the man's back. Mitch reached for the slash zipper on his right breast, slid it open, and extracted the cuffs. They glinted in the cold moonlight. He walked over, bent, and snapped them expertly on the man's wrists.

"Don't move," he added. "Anything."

The man was motionless.

Mitch turned his attention to the one who had absorbed the laser twice. But he did so carefully. He was certain that both of these goons were capable of absorbing enormous quantities of pain; to take them lightly, he knew, would signal his imminent demise.

Grabbing the man by the back of his coat collar, Mitch lifted him to a rough sitting position and propped him against the bole of the willow. The man's leg flopped at a strange angle, he noted; he noted, too, that the blood seemed to have been stemmed there. The man was heavy and swarthy, and he bore his punishment well. His pale face was tortured, and angry; his teeth bared as he bit back sounds of his personal torment. Blood had caked on his lips and nose, but the whites of his eyes flashed alertly all the while. Mitch glanced at his hand. The baby finger and the ring finger beside it were missing, and the blood was flowing freely from a ragged, welling slash across the fleshy part of his palm.

Mitch studied the two figures, planning his strategy. He bent and quickly pocketed the laser that had sought to burn a hole through his chest, then he began a weapons search. Attached to the man's calf, under the pantleg of his torn, twisted limb, was a Viper Knife. The watertight, hollow handle, when popped open, exposed a forty-centimeter wire garrotte; there were also two tiny needles, their tips wrapped in adhesive. Mitch knew that their tips were fatal. Alloy handle, he thought, and stainless steel fifteen-centimeter blade. He added it to the laser in his pocket.

In a leather holster on the back of the man's hip, above his right buttock, Mitch found a "Star" pistol, the reliable Spanish-made weapon renowned for lightweight accuracy and reliability: 45 ACP, a ramp front sight, crisp trigger action, all polished blue. Mitch hefted it, feeling traces of familiar envy and anger surfacing. About 230 grams, with ammo. Nice. Bastard, he thought, trying to control the surge of sudden hostility.

It, too, disappeared into his pocket, which was now becoming bulky.

That seemed to be it. Mitch let the man sag back against the willow, his gaze pitiless in the dark. The man's right hand, minus the two fingers, was pressed tightly against his stomach, the blood spreading wetly into an amorphous stain. His teeth were still clenched harshly in reaction to the pain flooding throughout him.

Mitch turned his attention to the one on his face in the grass.

Walking to him, he bent and clutched him by his shoulders and slid him along the grass to within a few meters of his cohort. Then he rolled him onto his back and hauled him into a sitting position by the front of his coat. Stunned, the man nevertheless stared back at him, his anger and hate all too evident.

Mitch picked the lightweight plastic G.E. laser pistol from the grass where it had been dropped, adding it to the swelling arsenal in his own pocket. Then he turned and moved his hand up the man's calves as he pressed the butt of his Bausch & Lomb against the throbbing vein in the man's left temple; the man continued to stare at him, radiating waves of fear and odium.

Mitch smiled coldly back.

This one was loaded. Mitch suddenly realized what exactly had been stalking him, and how lucky he was to have them both submissive here like this. On the right calf: a military-issue Gurkha Kukri knife, a super-chopper with a half-centimeter-thick thirty-centimeter blade. Its sheath was the classiest Mitch had yet seen— leather, with wood lining and brass fitting. Undoing the entire assembly, he tossed it aside a few meters where he could still see it.

On the left calf: an aluminum telescopic blowgun, in a doeskin leather fitting, with six .38-caliber steel darts. The only place Mitch had even seen one was during a weapons exhibition and demonstration years ago in basic training. He recalled the stats now: speed, one hundred meters per second; range, seventy-five meters. He had seen it demonstrated and remembered how it had pierced two-centimeter plywood at maximum range. He undid it carefully with his left hand, fully aware that the darts would have poisoned tips, and tossed it beside the Kukri knife.

Mitch found another laser in a concealable shoulder holster. Larger than any he had seen before, it had a barrel about twenty-five centimeters long, with a retractable telescopic shoulder-rest so that it could be fired like a rifle. He rolled the smooth black plastic over in his hand: a Sanyo. Probably maximum heat and maximum range for a hand weapon, he thought. So this is the future, Mitch mused bleakly. When he saw the slots for attachments along its sleek barrel, he realized what it was missing. Dropping it into the grass behind him, he rifled through the man's pockets again as best as he could with his left hand only until he found it. A Nite-Hawk Scope, complete with tiny argon cylinder. Clipped to the Sanyo, it provided infrared death to total darkness, at phenomenal distances.

Mitch felt a cool belligerence sweep through him. "What will your boss say?" he asked suddenly.

The man was surprised at being spoken to. "Don't know what you're talking about."

"All this . . . stuff"—Mitch gestured toward the array of weaponry—"and *I* got *you*."

For a moment, the man could only seethe. Then: "Yeah. For the time being."

"No," Mitch said. "For as long as I want."

The man's brow wrinkled in a perplexed frown.

Mitch stood up, backed away a meter. Then he opened his coat and shifted the Barking Dog on his belt toward his navel, where it could get a proper sighting.

The man's eyes widened as he saw it, recognized it.

From his pants pocket, Mitch took out a small leather case and flipped it open. A circular glass cap about the size of a silver dollar, with a rectangular black vertical attachment, appeared in his hand.

"What's that?" The words had slipped out before the man could stop them.

"Scan-eye infrared viewer," answered Mitch tonelessly, screwing the cap onto the video-eye of the Dog. "The Dog wants to see your faces. All of them."

The man swallowed. "What do you want?"

"I told you. Information." The assembly completed, Mitch flipped the box closed and put it back into his pants pocket.

"This whole business is too big for you, Helwig. We know who you are. You can't get away with anything. You do anything to us . . ." He glanced at his partner. "Anything else . . . and you'll be taken out, permanently."

"By the Archangel."

The man said nothing.

"Watch." Mitch bent and retrieved the buffed black Sanyo laser. He slid the retractable shoulder-rest from its condensed mooring, tucked the laser snugly into his right shoulder, then turned and sighted it on the man propped against the tree. Even with his face clotted in blood, and through the haze of pain emanating from his leg and hand, the stranger came to full awareness as Mitch leveled the laser at him.

"Can you give the Dog any reason why I shouldn't kill you?"

The man just stared at him.

"Any reason at all."

"Because if you do, we'll get you!" the man in the cuffs screamed suddenly from beside him.

Mitch turned his head to glare at the one whose laser he now controlled. Then he turned back to the injured man twisted at the foot of the tree. "Bullshit," he said.

He squeezed the trigger.

A bolt of light with a blue shimmer to it erupted from the mouth of the Sanyo and tracked instantaneously onto the chest of the man at the foot of the black willow. Its power, Mitch realized as he held the trigger down, was devastating. The man made no sound as he died. The hole in his chest grew to the size of a fist, and his eyes and mouth gaped openly when Mitch finally released the trigger, having burned the heart to a bubbling vapor. Blood welled freely from the smoking cavity, flowing toward the cold, silent earth.

Mitch turned away from the man he had killed and methodically studied the stunned visage of his remaining captive. The man's hardened features had been transformed from the texture of carved apple to mashed potato in the last few seconds. Good, thought Mitch. Very good. He had used his two-man advantage as dramatically as he could, and now it was time to see if it had paid off. The look on the man's face told him he was close.

"Jesus Christ," the man muttered.

Mitch held the Sanyo at a calculated half-mast. With his left hand, he spread his jacket open so that the Barking Dog could see the man clearly.

The man's eyes were wild now, darting from Mitch to the body of his partner and back again. He was anticipating his own death, and wasn't handling it very well. Not nearly as well as he handled his victims' deaths, Mitch reflected bitterly.

"What's in the warehouse?"

The man licked his lips. "You'll kill me whether I tell you or not."

"Maybe not."

The man was silent for a minute, running the whole horrid skein of possibilities through his fevered brain. He didn't like any of them.

Mitch began to raise the Sanyo.

"Wait! Wait a minute."

Mitch shrugged the butt of the shoulder-rest comfortably into position. "Why?" He ran a finger down the burnished shaft of the weapon.

"I'll tell you. I'll talk to you."

It was the truth. There was no telltale shiver from the Barking Dog.

Mitch took his time lowering the laser, not wanting his acquiescence to seem too quick. A sheen of perspiration had sprung out on the man's upper lip, in spite of the cold night.

The Sanyo came to a halt once again at half-mast, never completely leaving the scene—or the man's imagination. The stranger risked a glance at his dead partner, licked his lips in fright and shock, then let his weakened eyes meet his captor's.

"What's in the warehouse?" Mitch asked again.

"There's . . . there's all kinds of stuff in there," he stammered. "It's a storehouse for goods that need to be fenced, or disguised, or just given time to cool down. There's . . ." He stopped, looking at the Dog, then continued, "Drugs, automobiles, guns, stuff like that."

It was all true. But Mitch knew that they hadn't scratched the surface yet. It would take more questions, and more answers.

And fear. And uncertainty.

"Tell me about the drugs."

"I don't know much."

True.

"Tell me what you do know. Tell me something interesting."

"Mostly coke." He spoke more quickly now. "It's easy to store, easy to move."

"How much is in there?"

"Don't know."

A flash of cold illuminated Mitch's side. He began to raise the laser.

"Wait! I mean I don't know the exact amount, or the total amount, really! I have some rough ideas."

"Like?"

"Like, several tons—"

"Tons!" It was true.

The man shrugged. "I've been trying to tell you—these are the Big Boys. They're not gonna risk their operation for one guy, a cop like you. You'll be put away when they find my partner—and if you kill me. Listen"—he tried his angle—"you can still get out of all this. I'll make a deal with you. We'll work out a plausible story about what happened to him," he said, nodding in the direction of the corpse by the tree. "You can still walk away from all this. It's not too late."

Mitch pretended he was considering it. "Tons of coke," he repeated. "One ton's worth about five billion on the street. How many tons?"

"I've seen five personally. I understand there's more."

Mitch was stunned. No wonder we can't dry up the streets, he thought. "Is it manufactured on the site?"

"Not that I know of. It's all Colombian—best stuff."

"How do they get it in?"

"Lots of ways. But I don't really know much about it. It's not my line."

"What is your line?"

"I look after Mr. Scopellini's personal interests."

"Him, too?" He indicated the dead man.

The man glanced at the body automatically, then swung his eyes away swiftly. "Yeah. Him, too."

"Not very good at it, are you?"

The man said nothing.

"Tell me more."

"Like what?"

"There were six thousand lasers stolen from the Moss Park Armory recently." And seven men murdered, he added to himself. "Are they in there?"

The man hesitated, then nodded.

"I couldn't hear you."

"Yes."

The Dog did not bite. Mitch's brain was beginning to reel as he considered the magnitude of his find.

And this is just one city, he thought suddenly. Is this going on in all the other cities of the same size? If it was true, and he suspected it had to be, police forces were sadly overmatched, in awesome proportions. And in his heart, he knew it was so. He also knew what he had to do.

"There's something else."

Mitch was startled back to the present. "What?"

"Something you should know."

Mitch waited. The Dog waited.

"There's a dossier on you and your family being completed right now. The Archangel will have it by morning. He'll know everything about you. He'll know about your wife, about your daughter—"

"What about them?" Mitch's voice was razor-sharp.

"They'll be in danger if anything happens to me, and I don't cover for you. If we don't come up with the right story to explain all this away . . .'' His eyes were gleaming. He figured he had found the wedge he needed and had pounded it tentatively into the man standing over him, searching for the proper amount of force without cracking the subject of attention.

On the surface, he remained calm; but inside, Mitch boiled with outrage at having them mentioned at all—at even an implied threat. He contemplated the scum sitting in front of him, knew he couldn't let him get to him before he had milked him.

But the man continued. ''The Archangel oversees dozens of things. Most of them, I don't even know anything about.'' Thinking that if he told the man hovering over him about one particular facet of the Archangel's domain, it would shake his tormentor to his roots and might get him out of this hole, the cuffed man went on. ''He's into everything. You name it, he's got a piece. He's even going legitimate in some things—you know, portfolios arranged by lawyers, IBM stock, Bell Telephone, breweries, Xerox . . . But he's into the dirty stuff, too.''

''Like?''

''Prostitution. Gambling. Porn. Some kiddie porn. Even some snuff features.''

Mitch stiffened, his loathing rising.

''He uses girls . . . little girls, sometimes, for his snuff features. I know there's at least one suite of rooms set aside for that stuff in the warehouse. And when he's done with them, he uses their parts, their organs, for sale on a black market that's established for such items.''

Mitch's head was spinning. ''What're you talking about?'' It seemed to be moving too fast for him now. He had heard it, but a part of him was refusing to let it register.

''There's big money in it. Corneas, livers, limbs, hearts, kidneys, bone marrow, even testicles . . .''

It must be true, but Mitch couldn't believe it. He hid his shock from the Archangel's man.

"That way, he gets to salvage as much as he can from producing a snuff feature. Nothing is wasted."

Mitch managed to ask, "Isn't this all small potatoes, compared to the dope dealing?"

"He likes to diversify. Says it's good business. Says it demonstrates that a man has *vision,* that he won't be surprised by the future. He thinks the market for human organs will be one of the biggest in another decade. I've heard him talk about it. He wants to establish the market, so to speak, to be in on the ground floor. I think he sees himself kind of like the Al Capone of his era: the first, biggest, and most enterprising in new fields. *Vision.* It's one of his favorite words."

Nothing rang false for the Barking Dog.

"That's why I'm telling you all this, don't you understand?"

"No. Explain it to me."

"Your *daughter.* Your *wife.* Can't you see now what he could do to them? Can't you see it?"

Mitch felt himself expanding internally like a volcano about to burst and spew ashes and lava across the countryside and far out onto the lake. "You incredible fucking scum," he said.

The man's face froze.

Mitch raised the Sanyo to shoulder level and fitted it tensely in the crook there; then he aimed it deliberately at the figure on the ground in front of him. The man had been going to die tonight anyway, eventually. All he had done was hasten his certain demise.

His plan had backfired. It had been the wrong thing to say to Mitch Helwig.

The last wrong thing he would ever say to anyone.

As a gust caught the man's hair and whipped it backward, Mitch saw his eyes in the wan moonlight: the man knew that he had played the wrong card and that there were no more hands to be dealt.

The bolt of steel-blue light leapt from the laser and the

stranger's face disappeared into the hole that began between his eyes. Five seconds later Mitch released the trigger, blinding himself momentarily with the sudden plunge from incandescent brilliance into the black of the October night.

The image of what the man had suggested still floated like a specter in his mind. Mitch knew he would have to act tonight. There could be no more waiting. Not after this.

Not after what he had heard.

PART
THREE

*Nothing astonishes men so much as common sense
and plain dealing.*
—RALPH WALDO EMERSON, *"Art"*

*Our life is frittered away by detail . . .
Simplify, simplify.*
—HENRY DAVID THOREAU, *Walden*

Chapter 33

At 11 P.M. Arcangelo Scopellini thought about Helwig, his own personal dogged lone wolf, for the first time in two hours. That was how long it had been since Eveline had arrived and taken his mind so mercifully and skillfully away from the mundane nuisances that naturally befell a man in his position. She lay naked beside him now, curled in the pink satin sheets, smiling contentedly, her large eyes closed, her long-tipped fingers softly caressing his thigh. He sat propped up against the pillows and smoked a dark cheroot, recalling fondly the sensual passion he had just experienced.

Mewing, she snuggled closer, reaching up to cup him between his legs. The Archangel tensed under the pleasure of her expert ministrations, reaching down to run a hand across the smooth, soft skin of her shoulders. To his amazement—and delight—he found himself becoming hard again, found the memory of Mitch Helwig flashing off and on sporadically until it vanished completely as Eveline, sweet Eveline, brushed the covers from his lap, teased him with the feathery tips of her long fingers, and let her dark hair trail electrically along his thighs as she shifted to engulf him in her exquisite mouth.

He inhaled in a silent gasp as he reached over to extinguish his cheroot, clenching his teeth as his mind began to bob about in its own private pleasure pool. He tripped the switch beside the heavy, molded ashtray that activated the tinglers attached to the small of his back and to Eveline's breasts.

They moaned simultaneously.

As he put his head back into the lavish softness of the pillows, the Archangel's mouth opened and his eyes shut, and he thought of Mitch Helwig no more that night.

Chapter 34

At 11 P.M. Mitch Helwig parked his Chevrolet on Glen Manor Drive in the Beaches and strode up the walk to the darkened house. Without hesitation, he pressed the doorbell and waited.

A light blinked on in a second-story window; thirty seconds later, a hall light was switched on inside. And then an overhead light on the porch illuminated him fully to whomever was within.

Karoulis was standing in his bathrobe and pajamas and corduroy slippers when he finally opened the door. For a moment, neither of them said anything, waiting for the other to begin. Then the captain's rank took over.

"Come in, Mitch." He stepped aside.

Nodding his acceptance, Mitch entered and closed the door behind him.

They studied one another in the vestibule of the stately old home. Karoulis stared at the scorched hole on the chest of Mitch's jacket, his own eyes widening; then he looked at Mitch's face and into his eyes, noting the steely calm there.

"What is it?" Karoulis asked.

"I want your help."

Another moment passed in silence.

"Let's go inside." Karoulis turned and made his way through the oak and glass doorway into the living room. Mitch followed.

"Sit down."

"No. Thanks."

Karoulis shrugged. "Have it your way." Then, in a lower voice, "You usually do."

"Sorry to wake you up, Captain."

"You didn't wake me. I don't sleep the way I'd like to anymore." He looked at Mitch. "Do you?"

"No. But I'm trying to do something about that."

Karoulis opened an Oriental cigarette box on a Victorian end table and took out a cigarette. "I've been trying to quit this, you know." Placing it between his lips, he faced Mitch. "Lately I seem to get the urge whenever I confront you." His brow wrinkled. Pulling a book of matches from the pocket of his robe, he lit up, inhaling deeply, then expelling the smoke slowly. Finally, he said, "What can I do for you?"

Mitch paused, then asked, "Are you alone, Captain?"

"I am this week. Helen is in Montreal, visiting our daughter. She's in school there, at McGill. And I'm too old to chase other women. Does that answer your question?"

"Yes."

"And?"

"You know what I've been doing, don't you?"

Karoulis hesitated before answering this time. "Yes. I think so. Not all of it. But I think I understand."

"Why haven't you done anything about it?"

Karoulis took another drag on the cigarette. "That," he said, "is the million-dollar question. It's what I've been asking myself fifty times a day since I talked to you in my office that day."

"It's because you can see that I'm cutting through the bullshit. It's because you're swamped in a sea of bullshit, from morning till night, and you're tired of the taste. It's because, after thirty years of walking the line, after thirty years of wading in the muck, you're close to retiring, and you're not sure you've made a difference. You became a politician instead of a cop; it was forced on you. And because you're a decent man, you did the job in a decent way. But it isn't working, and you know it. *That's* why you left me

alone. *That's* why you didn't jerk my rope back. Because your way
had failed. You knew my way couldn't be any worse. In fact, you
knew, in your heart, that it was the only real way to gain ground—
that it all goes beyond politics. It boils down to common sense,
and what's right and wrong. It boils down to trusting yourself, and
a few others, and operating accordingly.''

"I won't turn you in, Mitch."

It was the truth.

"I want more than your neutrality. I want your help. I want
your endorsement."

"For what? For you to cruise around after hours exterminating
small-time scum? You don't need my help or endorsement for that.
All you need is my neutrality. You've got it!''

Mitch was breathing heavily now. "Suppose I told you I was
onto something big. That what I wanted to do was in another di-
mension from exterminating small-time scum. That I could make a
difference. That *you* could make a difference."

Karoulis looked at him skeptically.

"Suppose I told you that if you helped me tonight, my way, you
could accomplish more than you have in the last decade. Suppose I
told you that?''

Karoulis licked his lips. "What have you got?"

"I've got the Archangel. Do you know who he is?"

"I know who he is."

Mitch undid his jacket, let the Barking Dog gaze at the captain.
Karoulis's lips tightened.

"You're not on his payroll, are you?" Mitch asked.

Anger flared in Karoulis's face. But he saw the Dog and understood. "I thought we were talking trust."

"This is my life we're talking about. I have to be sure about
this." Mitch added, "I'm sorry."

"No, I'm not on the take from him."

The truth.

"But I have my suspicions about a few others. Others who live
much better than I do."

Mitch relaxed, let his jacket fall over the Dog's eye.

"Honesty doesn't amass much of a fortune," Karoulis said.

"And playing politics doesn't let you sleep well. So where do we saw it off?" Mitch remembered wanting to kill this man. He remembered wanting to kill the hideously insincere beast that had hovered between them, walling them off from one another forever. Dishonesty, he now understood, was a form of death, if never apologized for. It walled you apart as surely as if one of you had died.

As surely as he was walled off from Mario.

Karoulis, he was sure, had felt it all, too. It was why Karoulis had let him roam. It was why he was listening to Mitch now. It was his way of apologizing, of not wanting to wall himself up, of dealing with his own hurt, from whatever sources. The Barking Dog had unmasked this man twice now, and Mitch respected what he saw. And he wanted this man to respect himself, because he was worth an army of Archangels and politicians.

"I have the Archangel," he repeated.

"Did"—Karoulis hesitated, then asked it—"did the Archangel kill Mario?"

Mitch's eyes suddenly hollowed. "It doesn't matter anymore," he said.

And then Mitch told him about what he had—about the six thousand lasers, about the guns, about the tons of dope, about the trafficking in kids and porn and human organs and stolen automobiles and God knew what else, and Karoulis finished the cigarette and went on to a second and then a third as he and Mitch continued talking, and soon it was midnight.

Chapter 35

At 11 p.m. Elaine Helwig finally accepted that Mitch might not come home tonight. Where he was, she had no idea.

How, she asked herself, had all this happened? How had it all gotten out of hand? Try as she might, she couldn't pinpoint a definite turning point in their relationship. It had seemed to unravel imperceptibly, thread by thread, row by row, until the entire pattern needed reweaving, almost from scratch. Mario's death, she knew, had been perhaps the largest single factor in Mitch's dramatic personality change; after that, he had been quieter, less impulsive, and yes, less attentive to her and to Barbie. That had provided the most severe derailing; the other factors were small snags in comparison. But taken together, they had sent the two of them on their separate ways.

In the darkness of their bedroom, she opened her eyes, but could make out only dim forms of the familiar objects surrounding her. Smiling sadly, she recalled her reference to Plato's Cave that night she had dined with Don. And she remembered the night she had slept with Don.

Yet she felt no happier. She had had her passion, her risk, and she was no happier. The emptiness that had come with this realization had scared her deeply, suggesting as it did that there was no easy fix for her sense of alienation.

She remembered the lunch with Don the next day, and how she had felt soiled. It hadn't worked. It had not been the answer. Don was not the answer—certainly not Don, with his wife and two children and home in the suburbs. What future was there for them? She as his mistress? Or as the Other Woman who might eventually lead them both to lawyers, alimony, and inexorably to therapy and exhaustion?

And he hadn't even minded when she said they shouldn't see each other that way anymore, that it had been a one-time thing; in fact, he had looked partially relieved and handled it with grace and ease. Almost too much ease, she had felt, confirming her feelings that she was doing the right thing. Life was full of distractions. Donald Barbour had been a major distraction, arresting her at what she now perceived as a particularly vulnerable juncture.

Her eyes wandered across the ceiling over her head, seeing nothing.

Had Mitch found out about them? Was that why he wasn't here, now?

Impossible.

Then where was he?

Was *he* with another woman? She had to admit, it was the most likely conclusion. And there was the matter of the missing money from their joint account—which she had never confronted him about. Instead, she had soothed her hurt, exacted a misdirected and ultimately unsatisfying retribution with Don Barbour.

She rolled onto her side, her eyes still wide in the dark.

She didn't want to end up like Jan Prudhomme—separated, a single parent. But then, who did? Jan hadn't wanted to either. These things just happened.

Didn't they?

She had to admit, she didn't know how they happened. What I want, she thought, is for it to be like it was, like when we were married, ten years ago. That's what I want.

That's what everybody wants, she knew. But it doesn't happen. We get older. We change. Things change. People leave. People appear.

People die.

And people are born.

She glanced through the door into the hall, lit feebly by the bathroom night-light, and thought of Barbie.

The first thing I can do, she thought, is get myself back on track—establish some priorities. I've already agreed to see Jan tomorrow night after work, but after that, more time at home with Barbie, with my own daughter. That's where it has to start. For the three of us.

Around dawn, sleep claimed her. But when she awoke to the alarm soon after, she was still alone.

Chapter 36

"Did you hear Huziak talkin' this mornin'?" Mario was pulling at his moustache as they got into the cruiser.

"No. What about?" Mitch got in on the passenger side and closed the door.

"They arrested some lady—forty-eight years old—who'd worked at the Inn on the Park for six years. Her place is full of stuff she's stolen from the hotel. She told them she was goin' to start her own hotel." He chuckled, starting the car.

Mitch smiled and raised his eyebrows. "What'd she have?"

"According to Huziak, five crystal chandeliers, five hundred towels, about fifteen hundred knives, forks, and spoons, a hundred ashtrays, sixty pounds of butter—"

"Sixty pounds of butter?"

"That's what he said."

"Where does one keep sixty pounds of butter?"

"In the freezer, asshole."

"Of course."

"Like I was saying—"

"Sorry."

181

"Twenty coffee percolators, ten kettles, a folding bed, a toilet seat . . ."

Mitch began to giggle. "No toilet paper?" he asked.

"Huziak didn't mention it. Maybe inventory isn't complete. Maybe she used all the toilet paper she lifted."

They both laughed.

"It could happen, you know."

"Who am I to say it couldn't?"

"Exactly. Anyway . . ."

"There's more?"

"A bit more that I can remember. Sixty or so pounds of sugar cubes—"

"A lot of sixties."

"Maybe she's a numerologist. Maybe she's a conservationist."

"Maybe she's nuts."

Mario hooted. The cruiser eased up the ramp from the underground garage, swinging east.

"Also had around a hundred mugs, flowerpots, about a billion of them little soaps . . . And you know, nobody even noticed the stuff was missing."

"How'd they catch her then?"

"Two other cleaning ladies saw her dumping a bag of stolen goods in an incinerator and mentioned it to the manager. That was the start."

"Gonna start her own hotel, huh?"

Mario shrugged, still smiling. "Huziak says she's already got a lawyer, and the guy claims that she's suffered two broken marriages and stored the stuff away to gain a sense of security."

"All except the toilet paper."

"Maybe it was the *quality* of the security that she was searching for."

"Or maybe she just had to use it."

"You're so crude. So unrefined."

"Just think, Mario. If you were insecure, all the finery you could lift from Station 52 to shore you up."

"That's right. That's exactly right. About a million fuckin' paper clips I could have. And all the fuckin' elastic bands I could ever dream of!" He shook his head. "And what do I do? Pass it up. Can you believe it?"

"No. I can't. You're incredible."

"I know."

They cruised along Dundas, turned south on Parliament.

"We need coffee."

"Absolutely. There's one down here farther. We'll stop," said Mario. He paused. "I got another letter from Max Rosen."

"From Greenland?"

"Yup. Congratulated me on Tony's birth and all that. The usual. Told me that Greenland was a nuclear-free zone. Did you know that?"

"I thought it was a warmth-free zone."

"That, too, I guess."

"And a culture-free zone."

"You don't like Greenland, do you?"

"I can't understand anyone wanting to live there."

"Max likes it."

Mitch shrugged.

"How can Max like it?" Mario wondered.

Mitch shrugged again. "How can a beautiful, intelligent woman like Angela like you? There's no accountin' for taste."

"My magnetic appeal to members of the opposite sex is a matter of record. And legend."

"Greenland can make no such claim."

"Seems to me that big cities are the exact opposite of where either of us should want to live—with kids and families and all."

"Rural environments are overrated for their safety and happiness. You know that, don't you? Statistics don't bear out the myth of the rural idyll."

"Statistics. I don't believe that shit."

Mitch was quiet.

"I mean, I got Tony to think about now."

"I can't see an Italian living in Greenland."

"What about a Jew?"

"I admit it: I'm baffled."

Mario slowed at a stoplight, stopped. "You know, on any given day, seventy-five kids don't return home from school. Ten are killed."

"I thought you didn't believe statistics."

Mario ignored him. "Angela and I went to a film at the local school, organized by the Block Parent group. It said before kids turn sixteen, one in three girls and one in eight boys will be sexually molested. Don't you see what I'm getting at?"

"Yeah," Mitch admitted, sighing. "I do."

"It said that as many as two hundred million 'street kids' around the world are at risk of being drawn into kiddie porn, trafficking, and prostitution."

"You're going to drive yourself crazy, Mario."

"Yeah." He paused. "I guess so."

"There are no guarantees, I grant that. But the odds are against anything happening to you personally. Or me, for that matter."

"But you can up the odds by living in Greenland."

"Fuck the odds. You could also die of boredom in Greenland. Or freeze your ass off."

"You can do that here."

"But you'd be running away. You can't run away."

Mario pondered it. "I'm not so sure."

"Look," said Mitch emphatically. "There's a Honey Dip Donuts ahead. Do they have any of those in fucking Greenland? Eh?"

Mario smiled.

"Eh?"

Mario nodded. "Probably not."

"Well, there you are." Mitch spread his hands expansively. "That's civilization—right there." He was pointing now. "Open twenty-four hours. Civilized."

"It's your turn to go in."

"Oh no, it's not."

"Sure it is. I went yesterday, on Gerrard."

"Yeah, but I went three times in a row last week."

"You did not."

"I did."

Mario was unsure. "Did you?"

"Sure. But just to show you how fair I am, we'll flip for it. How's that?"

"Why not? Big-hearted guy that I am."

Mitch pulled a quarter out of his pocket, flipped it spinning into the air, caught it, then slapped it onto the back of his left hand. "Call it."

"Heads," Mario said.

Mitch lifted his hand partially, peering underneath. It was heads. "It's tails," he announced, slipping the quarter quickly off his hand and into his pocket.

"Hey! I didn't ever see it!"

Mitch mimed innocence with his face and hands. "Would I lie to you?"

"Over something as important as this—yes!"

Mitch chuckled. "It was tails."

"Right."

Mario angled the car into the parking lot of the donut store, parked it about twenty meters from the door. "It's cold out there, Helwig. Was it really tails?"

"Listen," he said. "You can flip the coin next time I'm driving, and I'll believe you. Okay?"

"You can bet on it." But Mario smiled as he said it. The twinkle passed from his eye to Mitch's, and Mitch smiled, too.

He got out of the car and walked across the lot.

It was the last time Mitch saw him alive.

Chapter 37

At 2 A.M. Mitch and Karoulis stood on the roof of Station 52 on Dundas Street, their hands stuffed in their pockets, their shoulders hunched against the cold, gazing up at the prototype Sikorsky HH-90B BlackHawk that was hovering above them. Their hair fluttered uncontrollably under the turbulence of the copter's rotors. Beside them, two men were attaching steel-centered nylon cables from the copter to the body of the skimmer.

Yet another man approached from the roof doorway, some thirty meters away. Mitch knew who he was: Berenson, the force's mobile equipment manager. He had met him briefly downstairs.

Berenson's teeth flashed in the darkness. "What do you think?" His words were shouted, but scarcely audible.

Mitch shrugged. He wasn't sure what to think. But he smiled his satisfaction.

Berenson accepted this and began to catalog: "Damage-resistant, four-bladed main rotor system, an upgraded drive system; a high-thrust composite tail-rotor; back-up control system combines computer interfaces with electro-hydraulic control actuators; she'll do forward at one-seventy-five knots, dive at one-ninety-five, go sideward or rearward at fifty-five. Pullouts at three g's, pushovers at zero g, and sixty-degree banked turns that equate to about three g's."

Mitch shook his head, baffled.

"The pilot will have night-vision goggles, and the copter will use infrared, computer-linked central front beams to make the way seem like noon on the 401 for him." Berenson then pointed to where the cables hooked onto the skimmer. "These clamps will be released with the push of a button by the pilot, as soon as you say so. Frequency's been set inside the skimmer. And this," he added, patting the skimmer affectionately, "is as good as she gets, too. Another prototype. Honda's given us three to test. This is its first in-duty run." He looked at Karoulis, then back at Mitch. "You're a lucky man."

Mitch raised one eyebrow. Karoulis glanced downward.

"I mean, to have this equipment," he added.

"I guess," Mitch acknowledged.

"Most air-cushion vehicles have an integrated lift/propulsion system in which a gas turbine drives both fan and propellor through gearing. Engine speed is adjusted to give the required lift, which is the critical factor, and the speed of propulsion is regulated by varying the pitch of the propellors."

"How's this one different?" asked Mitch. Except for a few surface modifications he had noted, it didn't seem to different from the one he used on his solo night rounds.

"This one's got two turbines, more sophisticated mesh-gearing, so that everything functions with greater synchronization. Stabilizers have been added to the corner thrusters, bleeding air from the plenum chamber. And in addition to the usual vertical tail fin, she's got these small horizontal tail planes which move bodily. You get maximum speed, perfect idling, quiet as a dormouse— and this son-of-a-bitch can almost leap tall buildings in a single bound. Most flexible ground-effect vehicle on or off the market today."

"It just may have to do that."

"What?"

"Leap tall buildings in a single bound."

Mitch lifted the skimmer's door and placed the large duffle bag that had been beside him on the roof's tarmac in the passenger seat. Having secured the skimmer to the BlackHawk, the two assistants in overalls backed away, awaiting liftoff.

"Anything else I should know?" Mitch asked.

"Lots, probably." It was Berenson's turn to shrug. "You know already about the continuous-wave CO_2 laser in the hood. Be sure to wear night-goggles if you use it. Don't want to burn out your retina at that close range. The RDX explosive charges you wanted are in that bag there.'' He indicated a leather satchel behind the driver's seat. ''There's a dozen—plus an extra—each one the size of a pound of butter, with digital timers built in. Pick your time, set them, then get the hell out of there. And I mean *far*.''

''Your man up above,'' Mitch said, motioning to the copter pilot. ''He knows what he's doing?''

''He knows what he's doing.'' Berenson paused. ''Do you?'' He held out his hand.

Mitch met his eye, then took his hand, squeezing it firmly. ''We'll see.''

Turning, he met Karoulis's eye. He, too, was holding out his hand. Mitch took it, clasping it solidly.

''Good luck,'' said Karoulis.

''Thanks.''

Karoulis wanted to say something else. Sensing this, Berenson walked out of earshot. The captain continued to hold Mitch's hand. ''Mitch?''

''Yes, Captain?''

''I will recommend you for promotion. You can count on it.'' Nothing from the Barking Dog. Mitch's face slackened.

''You can count on it,'' he repeated.

Mitch dropped his eyes. The copter blades beat incessantly at the chill air about them. ''Thanks,'' he muttered, inaudibly.

But Karoulis saw the word on his lips, and felt glad. Maybe, he thought, we can make a difference. Maybe.

If we get through this.

Their hands broke apart, and Mitch swung himself into the driver's seat, pulling the door down, sealing himself in. He gave the thumbs-up sign. Karoulis relayed it to the pilot above, then backed away.

Slowly, the cables linking the skimmer to the BlackHawk tightened, until finally they stood straight up like steel rods. For a moment, everything remained frozen; then there was an increase in the tempo of the rotors' beat as the skimmer lifted off the roof. Like a spider dangling by gossamer threads from some nightmarish hummingbird, the skimmer, with Mitch Helwig encased inside, slid upward into the night sky, fading into the darkness.

Within minutes, even the sounds had disappeared.

Alone, Karoulis walked to the edge of the roof and gazed out across the lights of the city. He felt better than he had in months. Maybe years.

As the copter lost altitude, Mitch donned his night-goggles. Then he tripped the switch on the dashboard radio, opening the line to the copter above.

The pilot's voice came out of the dashboard. "That's it, straight ahead."

Peering ahead and down into the rivers of lights, Mitch finally made it out.

The warehouse. Herrington Storage.

"Got it."

It was big enough to provide the illusion of a small runway from the air. They dropped farther, staying well above the power lines, angling toward the long roof.

"I'll let you know when," said Mitch.

They dropped lower, still maintaining a steady forward motion. This must be, thought Mitch, what it's like to try to land on an aircraft carrier.

"Just don't signal for release if you figure you're more than eight or ten meters above the rooftop. Too dangerous."

"Right."

They were flying low over residential Leaside, the houses dark. Maintaining speed.

Lower.

Lower.

Laird Drive.

Now.

He fired the skimmer's engines. They caught and idled.

"Release."

Mitch felt the clamps open, felt himself drop, then glide downward. He pumped the corner thrusters, waiting for the familiar ground-effect sensation, and angled the horizontal tail planes for maximum brakage. There was a moment of remote cold as he thought that it wasn't going to work—the instant between his adjustments and the tactile sensation of the skimmer's action upon the surface of the roof below him.

For a moment, there was nothing.

He dropped.

Then he felt it, and relief flooded through him. It had taken hold. He was hovering.

He was down.

The Sikorsky HH-90B BlackHawk was already dwindling into the night, out across the Don Valley, before swinging around and heading back into the city. Mitch had to hope that any eyes on the ground, or within the warehouse, would have followed the copter's noise. Since the whole operation had transpired without visible lights, the hope was that the skimmer had not even been seen. And why would anyone have been looking for it? The operation he had just taken part in had been a first. They hadn't even been sure it would work.

But it *had* worked. And he was here—inside the security fence—having avoided detection. And hopefully, with a way out over the fence, once the job was done.

He cut the engines, and the skimmer settled onto the roof. Popping the door, he let it float upward.

And he listened.

He heard what he wanted to hear: silence.

Stepping out into the night, he listened again. Still nothing.

Bending, he brought out the leather satchel from the floor behind the driver's seat, grasping it in his left hand. His right hand reached into his duffle bag on the passenger seat and withdrew the

Bausch & Lomb. Crouching, he ran toward the nearest edge and peered down.

There was no activity. Nothing.

He pressed the light on his watch: 2:20 A.M. Reaching into the satchel, he withdrew the twelve RDX bombs and placed them carefully in a row on the roof in front of him, like a mason examining a dozen imported bricks. Each one had been preset for a ten-minute countdown, once activated. All Mitch had to do was press the buttons. After he'd told him what he needed to do, Berenson had assured him that these were what he wanted. RDX, Hexogen, T_4, Cyclonite—it went, he had been told, by several names. Plastic explosive, four times more powerful than any dynamite. Then Mitch reached into the satchel and withdrew the dozen plastic propane gas cylinders—each one about fifteen centimeters in length, shaped like bloated Polish sausages. *Gas-enhanced RDX,* he thought. It had been used to assassinate the Israeli prime minister last year.

He extracted the roll of adhesive tape from the satchel next, and spent the next two minutes carefully bonding each "brick" to its own cylinder. This done, he sat back on his haunches and breathed deeply.

For maximum effect, he knew they all had to go off within seconds of one another.

He checked his watch again: 2:25 A.M.

It was time.

As rhythmically as a clock ticking off the seconds, Mitch pressed the starter button on each of the dozen bombs in sequence, so that at 2:25:12 A.M. he had nine minutes and forty-eight seconds until they began to erupt, just as rhythmically.

His hands felt sweaty.

The digits on each bomb blinked away, counting off the seconds.

Mitch left the first one where it was, but gathered the others carefully into the satchel, stood up, and scanned the vast rooftop.

Then he began to walk briskly, stopping and placing them in widely separated spots.

Six. Seven.

Another fifty meters. Eight. Nine.

Fifty more meters. Ten.

Then it happened.

The laser beam lit the night, slicing through the shoulder strap of the leather satchel, burning through his jacket, his shirt, stopping only upon encountering the Silent Guard. Mitch's hand darted for the broken strap of the bag, catching it before it could hit the roof jarringly and send him unceremoniously into eternity.

He made his decision at the same instant.

Lowering the satchel carefully to the roof, he clutched his shoulder as if he had been hit fully, and slumped forward in feigned death.

For a minute there was no sound—nothing. Then, through the night-goggles, he saw the torso of a man appear over the edge of the roof, hauling itself up via the rungs of a fixed metal ladder.

He waited until the man had stepped onto the roof before rolling quickly to one side and aiming his Bausch & Lomb. The needle of light flared to life, tracked onto the figure at the roof's edge. There was a muffled oath of anger and shock. Then the man slumped forward heavily on his face.

Mitch breathed in ragged gasps, all his senses alert. There was no doubt in his mind that the man was dead. The only question was whether or not he was alone.

He lay perfectly still. Listening. Watching.

Beside him, the digitals ticked away relentlessly.

Satisfied that the man had been alone, Mitch sprang to a crouch and scuttled across the intervening space to see for himself. The man was lying face down. Mitch turned him over with a shove of his foot, bent, checked his pulse, then went to the ladder and peered down.

Empty.

A lone watchman, it seemed.

Then he checked his watch again: 2:31 A.M.

Christ.

Running back to the satchel, he carefully pulled out the remaining two bombs and hurried off to place them strategically.

He checked again: 2:32.

He broke into a run, heading back along the roof in the direction of the skimmer. The run took him the better part of a minute. Gasping, he swung himself into the driver's seat and fired the engines. They hummed into life and the skimmer rose up on its air cushion. Now, thought Mitch, we'll see whether this baby can leap tall buildings in a single bound. Because if she doesn't . . .

He ran it down the length of the roof as if he were preparing for takeoff at an airport. The roof's edge loomed rapidly closer.

Closer.

He pumped the corner thrusters and she leapt out into the void. He flipped the switches for full lighting. There could be no secrecy now. He had to know where the ground was. *Had to.*

He was coming down. About seven meters to go.

He angled the horizontals.

Yes . . . yes . . . there . . .

He had it! He could feel the ground. The skimmer's nose tilted forward awkwardly, scraping briefly along the asphalt, and then it righted itself and Mitch opened the throttle.

At the same time, three large field-lights erupted to life, bathing the yard with glaring illumination.

Mitch accelerated across the yard, heading straight for the fence. It had been his intention to slow if possible and burn his way out with the skimmer's laser. But there was no time for that now. There was no time for anything.

He revved it to maximum. The skimmer screamed across the asphalt. When he got to within twenty meters of the fence, he pumped the corner thrusters with a sudden, wrenching spurt, then turned them on full, and the revs whined far past the red line as the skimmer rose off the ground, higher, higher, straining at three meters, groaning at four, shuddering violently at five—

—and then floated over the top of the fence, and angled down toward the ground, until it was back in touch with its normal physics and capabilities.

Mitch risked a glance at his watch: 2:34.

But how many seconds?

The skimmer was running full down Commercial Road when it began.

Mitch executed a horizontally sliding right turn onto Laird as the second explosion went off. Then the blasts rocked the night at one-second intervals for the next ten seconds. At Eglinton Avenue, Mitch stopped, got out, and watched the volcano of orange and blue and white and red flames as they roiled upward, howling with crackling rage at the cold night sky, belching clouds of expanding, boiling black smoke with the fury of a sleeping giant suddenly awakened.

Within seconds, the night was alive with the sounds of sirens. Karoulis, he thought, had kept them off-stage nicely, until just the right moment.

He glanced at his watch: 2:36.

There was still something left to do.

He got back in the skimmer and headed east along Eglinton toward the Don Valley Parkway.

Chapter 38

About five minutes passed before Mitch realized that Mario had been gone unusually long. Not too unusual, he thought. Just unusual.

He wondered whether to turn the engine off or continue to let it idle. Everything you read, he thought, contradicts everything else. I'm glad, he mused, that it's the department's gas I'm idling away, and not my own.

Immediately, he began to ponder the fate of his family automobile—the Chev—with its balding tires, its pitted grille, and its weather-faded paint job. He snorted to himself as he imagined the inevitable dialogue with the Firestone dealer: "Naw, it doesn't need steel belts for just toodling around town. Glass belts will do her fine . . ." And then he began adding up the cost.

Another two minutes passed. He fidgeted.

Still no sign of him.

In fact, thought Mitch, there's no sign of anyone, now that I think about it. No one's come in or out of the store since we pulled in here.

He watched intently for the next thirty seconds.

Still nothing.

The first warning signals shivered up his spine. Most of what flashed through his mind was the stuff of nightmares—cops' nightmares—the paranoia that was part of their survival mechanism. He dismissed it as nonsense, but it would not go away. Everything felt wrong.

Mitch cut the engine, stepped out of the cruiser, pressed the lock button, and closed the door. He was standing in the lot, still puzzled by the lack of movement surrounding the store, when he heard the shot.

It was as though *he* had been shot.

His bladder gave, ever so briefly, and he wet himself for less than a second down his leg before his reflexes could be controlled. Then he ran across the lot, unstrapping his Smith & Wesson as he went, tears of fear springing to his eyes. He saw Mario dead, he saw himself dead, he saw Angela and Elaine and Barbie and Tony standing at their gravesides, saw himself looking up from the oblong pit as they lowered the two of them down, felt himself reaching blindly across to Mario, but unable to find him, unable to touch him.

He ran faster, his eyes blurring.

Thinking about it afterward, he wondered how and why he hadn't acted sooner, why he hadn't read the telltale signals properly, how he could have been daydreaming so carelessly.

How? Why? The words paraded through his brain relentlessly, beginning in midflight across the parking lot. It was, he came to understand, the same process of inattention that was the culprit in the case of nearly every speeding motorist he had ever pulled over. If they hadn't been daydreaming, they wouldn't've been caught. It was that simple. There was no *why* about it.

Somehow, he knew that this was the biggest radar trap of all.

Gun in hand, he barreled through the glass door, ignoring any subtlety or caution. None of it was planned; his body was acting for him now, and he felt himself being dragged along, his brain afire within his skull.

The place was empty.

A door slammed, back in the kitchen.

Mitch stood frozen.

A car screeched to life from behind the store, plowed through an array of plastic garbage cans as it spun out of the laneway behind the store and careened onto the street. Another two shots rang out and Mitch suddenly found himself showered with broken glass as the front window collapsed in slow motion at his feet.

He dropped to the floor automatically; lying there, his mind reeling, he knew what had happened.

He knew.

"Mario!" The word screamed out of him by itself, shocking him.

Silence. Only his heart pumping, pounding in his ears.

"Mario!"

Frantically, he stumbled to his feet. Blood ran into his eyes. Wiping it off with his sleeve, he stared at it uncomprehendingly. *The glass,* he thought. *I'm cut.*

But there was no pain accompanying it, no fear for himself. He was all right. He could sense that.

"Mario!"

The room echoed.

He stood, shaking.

He knew.

The gun slid back into the holster and he walked behind the counter, through a door, and into the kitchen.

There were three bodies. One was the girl who waited on the counter and manned the register. One was a man—the baker. The other was Mario.

All had been shot in the forehead. Mario had been badly beaten first.

Mitch's bladder gave way again for a second. He couldn't move.

And then he realized that a lump in one's throat was much more than an expression, as he felt his gorge rise and settle, and his breath catch as he struggled for air.

Folding up on himself, he sat down on the floor, with the three of them, and let the grief wash over him in vast, aching waves.

That evening, alone on his balcony, he took a quarter from his pocket and flung it, spinning madly, far out into the night.

Chapter 39

"Where's Daddy?" Barbie asked. She chewed her cereal and watched her mother carefully.

"He . . . he went to work early today."

Barbie continued to chew her cereal, thinking. It was not true. She knew that. Daddy hadn't come home last night. There wasn't the shaving lotion smell in the bathroom. She could see his work boots on the tray in the hall, near the door. And Mommy looked terrible.

"Is Mrs. Chan going to make me dinner again tonight?"

"No, dear. No, she isn't. I've made arrangements for you to sleep at Lottie's. I'll be at Jan's till late this evening."

Barbie stirred her cereal idly with her spoon. Her mouth twisted. Then she asked it. "Has Daddy left us, Mommy?"

Elaine's face looked haggard as she stared at her daughter. "No, dear. Of course not."

Barbie made tunnels in her cereal, then made a dam. She looked at her mother, but said nothing more.

Chapter 40

Mitch elicited some attention as he cruised up the Don Valley Parkway in the prototype skimmer. But at this time of the morning, traffic was light, only a handful of other vehicles. Gliding along at one hundred kilometers per hour, York Mills was only minutes away. Mitch used dashboard control and set the gas-dynamic CO_2 laser embedded in the front hood on preheat, readying it.

The run along York Mills took mere minutes more. He looked at his watch: 2:52 A.M.

He turned right. Just a bit farther.

There.

He maneuvered into the driveway, pulled up beside the north wall of the luxurious house, and swiveled the skimmer sideways, so that the hood faced the stylish brick.

The preheat indicator on the dash blinked off. It was ready.

With a flip of a switch, the laser rose up out of the hood, like a submarine surfacing for battle—the sixty-millimeter cannon—poised, stoked, and ready.

He backed the skimmer up a bit more, jockeying it into optimum position. Then, even with the night-goggles, he squinted for protection.

You fucker, you.

His right thumb hovered over the activator.

It was only logical, he knew, that the doors and windows would be wired and motion-sensored. Any assault on them would undoubtedly alert him. Mitch didn't want that. Not at all. That left only the roof or the walls themselves.

His thumb pressed down forcefully.

The blinding shaft of light burst onto the wall, melting within seconds a hole its own diameter. Moving the directional shaft in his right hand, Mitch ate a circle two meters in diameter. The only sound was a hissing and bubbling, as the brick returned to its natural chemical elements, and beyond.

He let his thumb up.

The light blinked out and the instant darkness was blinding. Mitch let his retinas accustom themselves to the change. A cloud of smoke was billowing out of the hole in the wall, carried away into the night.

Reaching into his duffle bag, Mitch withdrew the Sanyo with the folding shoulder-stock, remembering what it had done on the island. Unfinished business, he thought. Then he took out the thirteenth RDX bomb, the one he had put aside for this later use—if the first mission worked. He slipped it into his pocket, carefully. *Just like the thirteenth apostle,* he thought. *Always an unlucky number.*

For someone.

The hole started at about waist height. With a running tumble, he could somersault through and land on the floor, without touching the edges.

In theory.

All he had to do was execute the plan.

He cut the engines and stepped outside. He hadn't realized he was sweating until he felt the cold air on his skin. Walking up to the simmering hole, Mitch peered within.

Nothing. And it had worked. It was where he wanted it to be— into the front hallway.

He reached gingerly into his pocket and lifted out the RDX brick, leaned over, and placed it carefully inside, and to one side. Then he did the same thing with the Sanyo, also shoving it off to one side so that it would not hinder his entrance in any way.

The heat at the opening was almost unbearable.

I'm not, thought Mitch, as young as I used to be. This better work.

He backed across the full width of the driveway, inhaled deeply twice, and started. From a crouch, it took only three long strides at top speed, and then he launched himself through the hellhole, landing on his right shoulder, and somersaulting awkwardly onto his back. His feet hit the thick carpeting with a muffled thud, and he lay there, breathing gratefully. I made it, he thought. Into the Archangel's maw.

Rolling onto his hands and knees, he crawled to the RDX explosive. He pulled back his sleeve and checked: 3 A.M. He took the bomb into the ample living room and set it on the floor in the center. Then he returned to the hallway and retrieved the Sanyo hand-laser, composed himself, and gazed up the winding flight of stairs.

Adjusting his goggles, he started up.

Such a big house for one man. He thought of his apartment in Thorncliffe, of Barbie in her tiny room, of their storage locker in the basement that had been broken into twice, so that they now did not dare leave anything of value there. The irony was not lost on him.

He looked in the first bedroom. Empty. The second one consisted of an office of sorts—desk, computer, handmade Chinese rugs and English leather sofa, elaborate bookcases replete with glass doors and leather-bound volumes. Mitch found himself wondering if the man was as well read as it might appear. An educated bastard, he mused. Or just a showy one. Or just a bastard.

There were three more bedrooms down the hall. Two of the doors were shut, the third slightly ajar. Mitch decided to try the third one.

He eased it open and peered into the gloom.

The Archangel. With a woman.

Mitch opened the door wide and stood there, staring. They were both asleep.

Extending the telescopic shoulder-stock, Mitch shrugged the

Sanyo into the nook between his shoulder and chest, his hand gripping the barrel, his finger resting on the plastic trigger. Then he flipped the wall switch beside the door, and a Tiffany-shaded ceiling fixture lit the room.

Even through the goggles, he could see that the sheets on the bed were pink. And satin.

The woman awoke first and sat up. Mitch's eyes were drawn to her lush, naked breasts, to her stunning blond beauty.

"Angel!" she said, shoving his sleeping figure. "Get up!"

There was a moment's lag as he came to, then he too sat bolt upright. With his hair unkempt and his belly sagging perceptibly over the edge of the pink satin sheets, he failed to seem either formidable or threatening.

Mitch felt his hate rising.

"Who are you?" the Archangel demanded.

Mitch didn't answer right away. His hand steadied the laser rifle. "I'm your fucking nightmare."

The woman cowered back into the pillows and sheets.

"You," Mitch said to her. "Get out of here before I kill you."

She seemed paralyzed.

"Get out of here!" Mitch screamed.

She vaulted out of the bed and stood there naked. "My clothes. They're downstairs."

"Put on a pair of his pants. Put on one of his shirts. Then get out of here. Now!"

She ran to the closet and pulled a shirt from a hanger. A pair of pants, far too big, followed. With one hand she held the pants up while she gazed down at her bare feet. "I need shoes," she said.

"Is that your Corvette outside?"

"Yes."

"Then get the fuck into it now, before I solve your problem by taking you off at the ankles."

She hurried for the door.

"And," he said, stopping her in her tracks, "you never saw me. You never saw anything. You know nothing. Understand?"

"Yes."

"Go."

She left.

The Archangel sat watching the scene, gathering his composure. "I can give you money," he said.

"Yes. You can."

A spark of hope leapt into the Archangel's eyes. His faith in the corruptibility of his fellow man had been confirmed once again. "Put that thing away," he said, indicating the laser.

"No."

"Very well then. If you insist. But there's no need to hurt me. I'm much more valuable to you alive." He essayed bravado, hoping to win this man, somehow. "I have friends, people who would be upset if anything happened to me."

Mitch smiled.

The Archangel didn't like the smile.

"Who are you?"

Mitch continued to smile.

"You're Helwig, aren't you?"

"Yes."

A flicker of fear jumped in the Archangel's eyes. "Where are Otis and Purdon?"

"Your protection?"

"If you wish."

"Dead."

"How did you get in here?"

"I'm your fucking nightmare, scumface. I burned my way in." He jerked the laser menacingly. "Just like I'll burn your fucking face off if you don't do what I say."

"I can assure you—you have my full attention."

"The problem with assholes like you, Scopellini, is that you have no *vision*."

Mitch smiled as the Archangel's face blanched.

"You think you see the future, but you only see a cable TV

version of it. You only watch bad formula shows, and gaze down sewers at your own reflection. You want to see the future?''

The man in the bed said nothing.

"If you bend over and look up your own asshole, you'll see your future."

"Let's talk money. Let's talk big money."

"You have no *vision*, Scopellini. But money—yeah—that's worth talking about. How much have you got, right here, on the premises?"

"Seventy—eighty thousand."

"Where?"

"In a safe. In my office. Down the hall."

"Let's get it." He motioned for the man to get out of bed.

"What about . . . my clothes?"

"A man with vision would have a pair of pants at his bedside, in case of emergency. Especially a man with your dubious lifestyle. I'm surprised at you."

The Archangel got out of the bed and stood naked before him.

"Get a pair of pants. I don't think my stomach can take that."

Scopellini went to the closet and took a pair off a hanger, slipping into them wordlessly.

"The money. Let's go." Mitch waved the laser at him.

The Archangel led the way, out the door and down the hall, stopping and turning at the entrance to his office. "You can have more than what's in my safe, you know. I'll take you to the bank tomorrow."

"How much can I have then?"

"Millions."

Mitch smiled. "Just open the safe."

They went into the room. The Archangel walked ahead of him to a corner of the room, stopped, and motioned to an easy chair. "It's behind here."

"Move it."

He moved the chair aside. At floor level, embedded in the wall, was a safe, about a meter square.

"If there's a gun inside, or anything like that, I'll kill you while you're only thinking about it."

There was a gun inside, the Archangel knew. But now he had decided against trying for it. His options were closing off. He didn't like what was happening—didn't like it at all. *Helwig*. Goddamnit! He had known this man was a headache. He had just underestimated how big.

He bent and began to twirl the dial on the combination. A few seconds later, he flipped it open, swung the door wide, and stood back, letting Mitch see inside.

"Get me ten thousand."

"What?"

"You heard me."

Stooping, the Archangel withdrew one bundle of bills, then turned and handed them over carefully. Mitch hefted them in his palm.

"There are one hundred hundreds in each package. Is that all you want? There are more packages here."

"This is a lot of money for a cop like me. It's all I want."

"I don't understand you. What do you mean it's all you want? I've offered you millions. You can retire to Europe, to South America."

"You could never understand me. You have no *vision*."

"What do you want?" The Archangel's teeth bared this time, in manic desperation.

"To burn you off the face of the fucking earth. Like a boil filled with pus. That's what I want."

"You're crazy!"

"How does that help you?"

Mitch jerked the Sanyo into position, aimed it, and said again, "You have no fucking vision, Scopellini." He pressed the trigger and the beam erupted from the barrel, the crystal blue death boring a smoking, bubbling hole in his chest. He left his finger on the trigger as the Archangel slumped to the floor, mouth and eyes open in death. Then he moved the beam up along the Archangel's chest and onto his face, collapsing his perfect Roman nose into his skull.

The hole widened, the heat rolled off him in waves, and in the vacuum of the Archangel's face, through his own misting, raging eyes, Mitch saw Mario Ciracella'a beaten and bruised face staring back at him. Dead.

It was then that he let the trigger go. Blinking, he gasped for breath, feeling drained.

Turning, he left the room, went down the stairs, walked into the living room, bent over the RDX. He checked his watch: 3:15.

He pressed the activator button. The digital began counting down. Ten minutes.

He was on the parkway when he heard the explosion. Glancing out his window, over his left shoulder, he saw the sky glow white and orange, and he felt tired.

It's over, Mario, he thought. *It's all I could do. I don't know what else to do.*

I just don't know.

And he cried.

Chapter 41

Karoulis was in his office, smoking a cigarette, when Mitch walked in at 3:55 A.M. He smiled when he saw him.

"I'm glad you're back," he said.

"I'm glad I'm back, too."

"Phone's been ringing off the hook here. I'm not taking any more calls."

"What do you figure will happen now?"

"Hard to say. Depends on how high his influence went—who was on his payroll. And since his payroll doesn't exist anymore, it's hard to predict whether or not people will be vocal or silent. My guess is pretty vocal."

"What'll happen to you?"

The captain shrugged. "Probably have to resign. We'll see."

"I'm sorry."

"Don't be. I'm near retirement. It was my decision." He paused. "Actually, I feel quite good about everything, all things considered." He looked at Mitch. "Strange, eh?"

Mitch shook his head. "No. I don't think so."

Karoulis exhaled a long cloud of smoke at the ceiling fan. "Maybe I'll go back to Greece."

"I don't think that's such a good idea. We can use you here. I think we're just starting."

They eyed one another appreciatively.

"We'll see. Let's just let it happen, Mitch. For now, for tonight, I just want to feel good, like this, for a while." He smiled.

"Want to go for a coffee?"

"Yeah. I do. That sounds perfect." He got up from his desk.

"I know a spot not far from here. Over on Parliament. We can go there."

Karoulis's eyes softened. "Yeah. I know the spot. Good choice."

"We can talk for a while."

"I'd like that. I'd like that a lot."

Chapter 42

When he heard the front door click open, Mitch checked his watch: 11:10 P.M. He was lying on their bed, his arms folded up behind his head, waiting. His stocking feet were crossed. He hadn't bothered to undress yet. In fact, he had spent most of the day lying there, thinking, since arriving home at noon. The note in the kitchen said that Barbie was sleeping over at Lottie Patel's. He smiled when he thought of Lottie, of her missing front tooth. He liked her.

This, he thought, is it. This is where I find out the truth about my marriage. The dogs are gonna bark, one way or the other. I spent most of our life's savings on this device under my shirt, just for a chance to finally know the truth. Just a bit of truth. Finally.

How many people get even that?

Mitch could hear Elaine taking her coat off and hanging it up in the hall closet.

His palms were sweating, his heart hammering.

The truth.

The truth was that he had married Elaine Barry ten years ago, that she had been a vivacious girl of twenty-four, that they had an eight-year-old daughter whom he loved more than his own life. That they had gotten ten years older. And they had weathered it. Even with his shitty cop hours, seldom home for dinner. Seldom home for anything, for that matter.

And the fluctuating interest rates, and the union demands, and the orthodontist, and Barbie's birthday parties, and their lovemaking—a wind that blew both hot and cool—and morning coffee in the summer and burned toast in the fall . . .

And Mario . . .

He heard her coming down the hall.

The electrode tickled his side, a hound deciding whether to whine and sniff or howl at the moon.

The truth.

As the bedroom door opened, Mitch reached under his shirt as if to scratch and pulled the electrode from his side. He let it dangle uselessly, a muzzled dog.

Elaine looked at him, but said nothing.

"I'm sorry," he said.

She looked in the mirror and undid her necklace.

"Where have you been?" she asked.

"Can we talk about it in the morning?"

She unbuttoned her blouse, pulling it free from her skirt. Then she turned to face him. "Yes." She was glad to see him. "I'm really tired. Jan is driving me crazy. What I want more than anything else is a shower and some sleep. Barbie's at Lottie's."

"I read the message."

"You look a bit tired, too."

"Yeah. A bit."

"I'm going to the bathroom."

The truth was, Mitch knew, that this woman, who was once the girl he married, came home to him, from wherever, cared for him, talked to him, and slept with him. He liked to see her undressing in their room. He liked to listen to her. He liked talking to her. He loved their daughter.

It was enough. It was more than enough. It was the truth.

When she climbed into bed with him, he snuggled close to her, her back to his front, and cupped her breast as he always did. And they slept.

At work the next day, Elaine punched their joint account code into her computer to assess the balance. She needed money for a new winter coat for Barbie.

For long minutes, she stared at the screen. Eventually, she sat back in her chair and gazed out the window, reflecting on the ten thousand dollars that had reappeared in their account yesterday.

Chapter 43

When the phone rang at 10 A.M., Mitch was slow in answering it. He left it off video. "Hello?"

"Hello, Mitch?" It was a woman's voice.

"Yes."

"It's Angela. How are you?"

He smiled. "I'm fine. How are you?"

"Not so bad."

"How's Tony?"

"Better. He asks for you. When are you going to take him to ElectroWorld? You promised, you know."

"I know. Tell him we're going. Tell him we're going Saturday. I mean, what the hell, eh?" He laughed.

"He'll be too excited to sleep till then if I tell him."

"Tell him anyway."

"I will. I'll mark it on the calendar."

"Do that."

"Actually, Mitch, I called because I've got a visitor here. Somebody who'd like to talk to you. He just got into town yesterday, and dropped over this morning."

"Oh. Who?"

"Max Rosen. An old friend of Mario's."

"Max Rosen! From Greenland?"

"The same."

"He's there?"

"In the flesh."

"Max is there?"

"Flip on your video. You can talk to him."

Mitch flipped the switch. Angela's face slipped out of the picture and a man's face took its place. He had thin eyebrows, full, rounded cheekbones, a dark moustache, and a familiar smile. Mitch knew immediately why Mario and Max had been friends. He recognized the smile.

Mitch smiled back. He felt foolish at first. "Mario spoke about you, Max. You were his good friend. He made that clear." He shook his head in wonderment. "I'm delighted to meet you. I wondered if you were a figment of his imagination for a while. I mean—Greenland!"

Max laughed. Even the tone of the laugh was familiar. "Yeah," he said. "Greenland."

"I'm sorry about Mario, Max."

"So am I, Mitch. We all are. You were his best friend."

Mitch said nothing.

"He said so in every letter. I've wanted to meet you. I knew that if he liked you, I'd like you, too."

"I'm glad you called, Max."

"*I'm* glad I called."

"Are you in town for long?"

"We're in town for good, Mitch. We're moving back. Or, at least, I'm moving back. My wife is just moving."

"I thought you loved it in Greenland."

"I did. For a while. Then I got bored. Besides," he said, "I'm not sure it's a good place to raise a kid. I'm gonna be a daddy soon."

Mitch smiled, kindly.

"You know?" Max said.

"Yeah. I know."

Max shrugged. "So we're gonna try it here. Who knows? Maybe we'll get bored here, too. Maybe we won't like it. How can you tell?"

"All you can do is give it a try."

"Exactly." He glanced sideways, presumably at Angela, then back at Mitch. "Besides, if you think it's cold *here* . . ." And then he laughed.

"What are you gonna do? I mean, have you got a job or anything?"

"Not yet. But I'm looking. Something'll show up. My father wants me to sell furniture with him, on the Queensway." He rolled his eyes.

Mitch was thinking. "Can you and your wife come to dinner this weekend?"

Max smiled, shyly, but thankfully. "I think we could squeeze it into our hectic social calendar."

"Let's make it Saturday then. After I get back from ElectroWorld with Tony and Barbie. And bring Angela."

"All right."

"Seven o'clock?"

"Seven it is."

"Great. And Angela's got your phone number? Your address?"

"We're staying with my parents till we get settled."

Mitch smiled broadly. "Thanks for calling, Max. And thank Angela for me, too."

"I will. She's right here, listening." He glanced at her. "She thanks you now."

An hour later, alone, he set up his Quasar video camera on its tripod, focused it on the sofa, set the mike on the end table, pressed Record, and sat down. He made seven simple statements, spacing them about thirty seconds apart. When this was done, he got his Barking Dog from his duffle bag, propped the shiny rectangle in front of the TV, and attached the electrode to his left side.

He inhaled deeply, calming himself.

It didn't work. He tried again. There . . . a little better.

He leaned forward, flipped the TV on, pressed Play on the attached video recorder, settled back, and waited for his own image and voice to appear. It began.

"I want to know if Elaine was at Jan's last night," he heard himself say. Ice formed in his left side, burrowing inward.

"I want to kill scum like the Archangel." Nothing. True.

"I want to be a cop." A tremor, a shiver of uncertainty. Indefinite.

"I want to be promoted next month." Nothing. No reaction. The truth.

"I trust Karoulis." Nothing. Mitch nodded with relief.

"I want a partner again." There it was again: the shivery tickle of uncertainty. Good enough, thought Mitch. Good, honest uncertainty.

Mitch suddenly understood the pope.

"I want Mario back." Not a tingle—the unwavering truth. Mitch swallowed, feeling cleansed. The catharsis seemed complete.

In ways that Mitch had never anticipated, his Barking Dog had indeed helped the world emerge in clear, vivid images. He finally knew what to do. It was so simple.

At 2:30 P.M. sharp, Mitch was sitting in his Chevrolet outside Thorncliffe Public School. When the recess bell rang, he stared at the door through which he knew Barbie would have to emerge. He got out of the car and stood there, filling his chest zestily and smiling.

There she was. She was with Lottie, smiling and giggling.

"Barbie!" he shouted, waving.

She looked up, puzzled, then smiled and waved back. "Daddy!" she cried, then ran to the steel wire fence that separated them. "What are you doing here?"

"I'm on my way to work, sweetheart, and was just passing by," he lied. "Wanted to ask you a couple of things."

"What is it? Anything wrong?"

"No, no, nothing's wrong. Say, you remember that guy that

was shot out of the cannon at the circus you went to with your class?''

"Sure, I remember.''

"Well, we never did finish talking about him, and I got to thinking . . . What do you think he thinks about as he's flying through the air?''

"What?'' she said. "Daddy''—her eyes were rolling and a corner of her mouth was twisted wryly—"you are sometimes truly weird.'' She placed her tiny hands on her bony hips in a stance intended to convey her mock concern and tilted her head on a jaunty angle.

"It seemed like a good question to me,'' he said with equally mock seriousness.

"You came to school to ask me what I think the guy thinks about as he flies through the air? Really? I mean, *really?*''

"Best question I could think of,'' he replied, shaking his head.

"Well . . .''

"C'mon, c'mon . . . I got to get to work.''

"I think he wonders if he's going to land in the net. What do *you* think he thinks about?''

"I think he thinks about''—he looked from side to side, playing the game of imparting information that might violate the National Secrets Act—"what an absolutely, fantastically lucky guy he is to have a clever, beautiful daughter.''

She beamed and blushed simultaneously. *"Daddy!* You're teasing me!''

"No. I'm not. It's what I think. But enough of him. One more question, then I'll let you go.''

"Yes?''

"Do you love me?''

Barbie clucked her tongue and rolled her eyes again. "You *know* I do! Silly . . .''

It was true. Mitch did know it. It was the one thing he knew without a Barking Dog—knew with a certainty that Pope Martin would have envied. It was the only thing, he had realized after listening to his own litany of statements this morning, that he had never doubted.

"I love you, too," he said. And this, too, was true.

He waved to her as she stood, separated from him by the steel wire fence and years of innocence, and she waved back. From now on, he thought, I'll try to be my own Barking Dog.

If I can.

I know, he thought. Yes, I know what he thinks about as he's flying through the air.